the SILVER PENTACLE

Volume Two

Airship 27 Productions

™

the Silver Pentacle Volume Two
© 2023 Nancy Hansen

Published by Airship 27 Productions
www.airship27.com
www.airship27hangar.com

Interior and cover illustrations © 2023 Guy Davis

Editor: Ron Fortier
Associate Editor: Gordon Dymowski
Marketing and Promotions Manager: Michael Vance
Production designer: Rob Davis

ISBN: 978-1-953589-50-7

Printed in the United States of America

10 9 8 7 6 5 4 3 2 1

the SILVER PENTACLE

By Nancy Hansen

Volume 2
Table of Contents

LORDS OF THE DEEP

Roan Finnman

"Get gone, ye blasted freak, or I will lay ye out and skin ye alive!" The old man's voice was raised in anger and he backed it up with another volley of missiles.

As a barrage of small stones, lobbed by a large and sometimes deadly slingshot whizzed over his head and plunked all around him, the slender and dappled form of what appeared to be a naked man raced away with his day's plunder—a drawstring bag of small fish and a couple of crabs, which were a real delicacy. Running, he transferred his booty to one hand before leaping up off the end of a rickety wharf built of whatever materials were available. He twirled a bit in midair to show off before diving deeply into the cold and mucky brackish water, striking out to the safety of a sheltered spot only he knew.

Roan actually felt a bit guilty about stealing from the fisherman, but he knew the old salt had plenty of smoke-dried fish set aside and would only have sold these. Roan could certainly catch his own fish, but not in any large number, and chasing them underwater took a lot of energy. For over a decade now, he had been cruising up and down the drowned coastline, hiding out on the tiny islands that were once major land masses but were now just the high points poking up through the dark water. He eked out an existence robbing crab traps and fishing villages of their catches, or picking shellfish off rocks in order to eat regularly.

Winter would soon be coming, and the colder water meant he'd need a thicker layer of fat beneath his sleek, dappled skin covered with a fine pelt of plush, silken fur. Fingers and toes slightly webbed and adapted for swimming helped him paddle along the bottom of the bay more quickly. Roan carried the bag in his teeth and held his lungs closed long enough to clear the shoreline before surfacing for air. No land-walking humans had come out in boats to chase him, and he grinned happily as he yanked the sack's string over his head to hang around his neck before striking out for his current home.

What used be a high cliff crowned with a lighthouse atop had become an up-thrust rocky mass with a spit of stony beach and an abandoned old building rotting away. No one came near the shoal for fear of foundering a boat, so it made a good hideaway. Roan could sit on the wet rocks below the crumbling building and feed himself at leisure. There at least he was safe from the possibility of being hunted down, for he could see for miles around. At the first indication of danger, he could be in the water and away before anyone approached. A few seabirds still nested there, and some of them started squawking and complaining as he approached.

He bobbed along the shoreline, and threw his bag onto the rocks first, then heaved himself out, sitting down in the sun and salt spray to eat. The crabs first, they were sweet and juicy, and would not keep long. He kept a favorite rock handy, rounded on one end, pointed at the other, and hit one crab in the back of the head to kill the wiggling thing, then smashed it open and picked out the fresh meat and roe. The fish were no problem, most of them were already dead, and he simply ripped them open with his teeth and ate what he wanted, tossing the remains into the outgoing tide for the gulls to find.

Deciding he needed a rest after eating, Roan curled up in a dry sunny spot and closed his eyes, but all other senses remained alert in case something approached. The birds would likely warn him anyway, which is why he didn't take their eggs and eat their young. Other than the occasional shark, it was the humans who were the biggest threat this close to the mainland.

They knew Roan was not one of them, but something different. What that was, even he wasn't really sure. His mother certainly had been human, but he never met his Da. Chased away by her people after she died, Roan lived by his wits in the sea, the only place he felt truly at home. His mother had recounted to him the story about his father and his birthright many times, with her sad blue eyes full of sorrowful tears at each retelling. Now that he was an adult and had learned more about the world he lived in, Roan thought his Da must have come to Earth with the first influx of 'The Others From Elsewhere' that everyone was always going on about in their tiny coastal village. Roan recalled the villagers' whispers and their suspicious sidelong looks at him, and he felt very sorry for his poor mother, who had always felt shunned and tainted, and so was often alone.

"A grand selkie he was, Roan!" She had told him the story of their meeting as far back as he could recall. "A bonny prince of the sea, like in the old tales. I used to come down to the water's edge to scout for seals, for me own Da hunted them when he could. The skins were warm and brought a fair bit of trade. We started seeing selkies out there after the big wars, when the skies opened up at times and the things of fairytales and nightmares came to ground." She would always shudder at the thought. "The world changed then, for all of us." She would sometimes get choked up with all those memories.

"A selkie man came ashore one day. I saw him sitting on the rocks, his skin peeled back and laying about his waist. I was singing a little song as I walked along, and he turned to look at me, and oh, you know my maiden heart just melted! He was so handsome it made me gasp. Your Da, he always had the most beautiful big brown eyes I have ever seen, and the loveliest, most compelling voice when he called out to me. His hair hung damp about his shoulders, but it shone like brown silk of the softest, finest texture I had seen in the markets back in better times. When he smiled it warmed me cheeks red with blush to think it was for me. But as I drew close he took up his skin, pulled it on, and jumped into the sea. A coy one he was, and cunning too. He stole me heart from that day."

She would always stop there, remembering, and her thin, drawn face with the wild blue eyes shining, would look back to another life.

"I saw him many times, and he always called out, but swam off if I got too close. I should have left it alone I s'pose, because the selkies are fey ones; but I sorely wanted him, with all me heart and soul, and so I thought about him all the time. It was one high summer night when I couldna sleep that I left me Ma and Da and the younger bairns, and I went down to the sea. And like it said in the old tales, I let me tears fall in, seven of them, and sure enough, my selkie man came ashore to me. He loosed his skin and I doffed me own clothes—shameless I was, but all innocence too— and we lay together happily, all night long. Such a gentle, loving creature he was, I was never a'frighted. He left me there at dawn to return to his home in the sea, and I cried until I fell asleep again. Someone came along and saw me sleeping naked in the sand, and told me Ma, and she come git me. Hoo, did I get me bum paddled red!

"We moved inland after that, and I never saw him again, though I come back down to the beach and searched all over. When you started to grow in me belly, me Da was so mad he liked to have kilt me. But I dinna care what anyone thought, not even when other people insisted me family must turn me out and send me away for birthin' a monster. I loved your Da then and I still love him now, and always will. You are part of him, my son, and part of me too, so I love ye for that, and now ye're all I have."

His mother had lived a hard life, and she died by the windy cold seaside, coughing blood from lungs so weak she could barely draw a breath without shaking her bones until they rattled. Roan had walked out into the water with her frail form in his boyish arms, and watched the tide carry her bony thin body out to drift away and maybe find the father he had never known.

A mere child of twelve revolutions, he had been on his own after that. There was no place he would ever be welcomed or accepted, as his strange appearance—a combination of selkie and human—marked him as a monster in most eyes. He was not a selkie as far as he could gather from his mother's oft repeated description, for his skin did not come off, and his spotted pelt was on to stay. It tended to thin out on his neck, and the fur on his face was very fine and close without much dappling, so that it was only noticeable up close. Roan's eyes were wide set, large, brown and liquid like his father's, but they had the faraway sadness of his mother. Like his father, he had a fascination with comely and lonesome human women, but unlike him, he didn't have the same ability to mesmerize them, and that had almost gotten him killed a few times.

As a boy Roan had traveled all along the shrinking frozen wastelands to the north, following the remnant of what was once a vast community of thriving sea life along the sunken coast of the great continent. Now that he was a man there were few game fish of any size left in the area except for the big predatory sharks that hunted humans, for most of the larger edible aquatic creatures had died off or moved to deeper waters. The coastal people made some living scavenging mostly small things like mollusks, trash fish, and crabs. Roan stayed close to shore and waited until the boats came in, and simply helped himself to whatever it seemed the humans could spare. It beat having to outrun the big sharks in order to find enough to eat.

~

Happily asleep in the sun with a full belly and the precious memories of his mother's tales, he heard the dolphin before he saw her. Roan sat bolt upright and looked around. There hadn't been any of her kind in his waters for many seasons. He had always liked dolphins, they were playful and intelligent, and he was desperately lonely. He got to his feet, yawned and stretched, and clearing the rocks, leapt out into the water.

Taking an initial deep breath, he ducked his head under and called to her in an approximation of her own language of high pitched whistles, whines and squeaks, some above the auditory ability of human ears. "Where are you?" he asked.

Here, hurry, tangle, she called back frantically and continued to click and whistle. He swam out in the direction she called from, and cast about in circles, finally locating her by following the echo location clicks. She was quite a ways out, floundering and adrift a short way below the surface, her tail and beak enmeshed in a castoff net. Roan had no knife or anything sharp to free her, so he did the only thing he could think of. He gnawed at the rope with his teeth until he could loosen her enough to bring the entire mess to the surface, where she could spout and take a new breath.

"Are you all right now?" he asked in a worried tone.

Better, she whistled. *Breathe good.*

"I'm glad. Just let me get the rest of it off," he told her, hoping she would stay calm. The dolphin waggled her body lazily, just enough to stay afloat, but the movement made getting her free that much harder. Roan wished he had a knife, for it would have been so much faster to cut the net off her, but he no longer wore clothing so there was no place to put it. He worried away at the netting with his teeth, and though rotten, it was thick cording and it took a while to work his way past each strand. Eventually though, he was able to break through enough of them to set her loose, and he tossed the mangled remains far away.

"There. You're free at last," he said, patting her slick hide.

The dolphin whistled in appreciation. *Free good!* She said and clicked a few times happily. *What creature you?* She wanted to know.

Roan was at a loss to answer. "Selkie and Human together I think, whatever that makes me," he added with uncertainty.

Finnman, said the dolphin. *Swimmer mate with Landwalker always birth a Finnman.*

He supposed that was right, but had no idea, for his mother had called him Roan because of his spotted furry hide, and that was the only name he knew. Some of the humans had surnames—secondary titles they went by, and Finnman seemed as good as any. "I am Roan Finnman," he told her proudly, and the dolphin swam circles around him clicking and chattering in agreement.

Roan good sound, easy name!

"Do you have a name?" he asked her abruptly, and felt rather than saw her hesitate to answer.

Landwalkers give name, she said, rolling sideways and showing him a tattoo with some symbols on the underside of one flipper. *Click to me sometimes, but talk box fall off so now just name and no clicking. Pods not make names, just calls,* she explained further, hoping he would understand. *My call this,* she said, doing a long string of echoing squeals and chatter that ended in a few squeaks and groans.

Roan recognized the tattooed symbols as numbers and something indicating the military. "People—I mean Landwalkers—they did that to you?" he asked unhappily.

Yes, the dolphin said without any emotion. *I find the tick ticks for boats and tell Landwalkers. Many my pod die finding tick ticks that make big boom. Some live but swim wrong or not ever hear calls again. Not like tick ticks.* She seemed sad. *Pod is lost now. All dead. All gone into blood and meat. Now just me.*

Roan had seen warships before and knew all about floating mines and attached bombs. "The wars are mostly over for those of us who live in water," he said gently. "I don't know how to pronounce your name like your friends in the pod would, but you are free from the wars and free from the net, so I will call you Free, and we can be friends," he said entreatingly.

FREEEEEE! She squealed happily. *Is good name! I like be free, I like be friends. Friends go find good fish now! Free find food with you.*

She gave him the toothy dolphin version of a smile and they set off to hunt together.

Suddenly Roan's world was not so empty after all.

～

Roan and Free stayed together all through that rather harsh and stormy winter, traveling up and down the coast. When the seas were roiling and the gales blew up choppy waves, the dolphin could dive deep and swim away until she found calmer waters to surface in. He could have done the same, but his life was more tied to the world of mankind. As fast as he was, Roan didn't think he could out swim the big, hungry sharks and other monsters that prowled the open sea. So he shivered through most of the storms in the scant shelter of icy shorelines or huddled in tumbledown old fishing shanties that leaned drunkenly out of kilter atop rocky islands, some of which were actually the roofs of sunken high rise buildings, or flotsam peninsulas lashed by cold foaming waves. It was a miserable existence, but he survived by his wits. When the latest storm passed on, Free was always there to greet him with her clicks, whistles, and athletic jumping.

Getting enough food to eat was always a problem, for as active as Roan was, he burned energy at an alarming rate. Unlike his selkie parent, the half-human could not put on a thick enough layer of adipose tissue to tide him over through the cold months, and tended more towards the raw-boned leanness of his mother's family. He also didn't have the thicker selkie coat. Any extended span of bitter weather took a lot out of him, and even with Free's help hunting and whatever he could steal from the humans, by ice-out he was looking rather ragged and thin.

With the thaw came the fishermen, and other sea hunters took to the water again. No creature of the foam was safe. The humans hungered as much as he did, and they used whatever they caught and didn't eat for barter to get the things they needed.

Roan could pull himself up onto any inaccessible rocky isle and hide, but Free was safer out at sea. She wanted to stay close to Roan, but he was a coastal creature, and she was more suited for the deep waters. She had several narrow escapes with nets and gunners before she started roaming farther out.

Free eventually found a small pod to join with, and was thinking of taking a mate. It only made Roan feel more alone, for the wild dolphins seldom came toward land, where gunners might shoot them for meat. He saw less and less of her every day until they parted company for some months. She came back from time to time, but mostly he was alone, and without her company, he felt like more of an outcast than ever before.

$\sim$

One early spring day Free swam in fast and circled Roan, chattering like crazy. *Ship comes!* She called out to him in an excited tone. It was not a big surprise, as once the worst storms broke, traffic on the seas increased.

"What kind of ship?" Roan asked her, after surfacing long enough to scan the horizon. Some days before there had been a big fireball in the sky well out to sea, and they had both expected an attack of sorts, so it was wise to proceed with caution.

Big ship, she answered vaguely. *Hum hum sound, long, low. Maybe have boxes things. Maybe have inside load. Not know much. Too far away.*

That should be a cargo ship. The first one of the season headed for New Brooklyn. Roan wanted to see it for himself. Sometimes they threw garbage or ballast overboard and that drew fish and other scavengers, making hunting a meal easier. He was hungry as well as just plain curious.

He thanked her and watched as she swam off to rejoin her pod, and then headed toward the harbor to watch the freighter come in.

There were always ships in New Brooklyn Harbor, though far less in winter, because of the storms. The big ones stayed out on the sea docks for inspection per orders of Columbiana's Naval Authority, for far more dangerous things than non-native invasive plants and animals stowed away on them. The shoreline area was too shallow for the long, deep draft boats anyway, for what had once been a former coastal metropolis was now a watery graveyard full of bombed out skyscrapers, submerged bridges, and other crumpled creations of humankind.

Whatever series of cataclysms had plunged the big downtown area beneath the waves happened long before Roan's time. He would occasionally swim through the underwater wreckage, amazed that such a thriving hubbub of mankind had been reduced to sunken rubble that was gradually becoming a cold water reef. Roan often wondered what that world had been like, though it was so long gone under, none could recall.

It was a dangerous place though, for large, hungry sharks prowled through the once bustling streets and hid in and around the underwater canyons formed by submerged buildings, always looking to ambush something or someone. Free would not come into that area because of them, as well as the seal hunters, who were always looking for sources of fresh meat.

Other things lurked down there as well. Things best not disturbed, as many a curious and less cautious treasure hunter who dared to dive down found out the hard way. No human had Roan's speed and agility in the water, and he had just barely outrun those deepwater others—with their long reaching arms and sharp, shredding beaks—several times. If not for the influence of the mammoth Harbormaster, they would have decimated shipping throughout the area, but he seemed to consider them a delicacy and so their numbers were kept under control.

The vessel that came sliding in to the long sea dock was a cargo ship named *Solstice*, for that much Roan could read from her battered side. He had followed her in and then scrambled out of the water to watch from a nearby sea cliff that was actually the top of a sunken and crumbled building. There was something very interesting about this particular ship, for it bore the blessing sigil of a sea god, and there were three people on the deck besides her skeleton crew of a few weary and battered bluejackets and the short, weathered mate who now captained her. *Solstice* had passengers, and Roan could sense they too were not quite human either.

The big ship had obviously been through some kind of battle, for the decks were scorched and bloodstained, and the remains of gun stands still stood ready. Racks of cargo were broken into, and there was a good sized dent on her port side where she had been rammed. Yet it was the trio who stood on the foredeck where the parasail mast was now empty who caught Roan's eye, for two of them were ladies of a kind he had never seen before. They had some quality of competence and purpose about them; just in the way they held themselves, along with their mode of dress, which was designed for travel and not terribly attractive. They also had an aura of otherworldly power. But the sprightly androgynous figure standing with them held Roan's attention the longest.

It was one of the Numen, a class of lower level deities his mother had babbled about meeting in her fevered dreams, though he had not really believed they actually existed before now. There was no mistaking it, for the nimbus around that one was almost blinding to Roan's wondering eyes and to study it he had to lower the protective inner eyelids he used underwater. Seldom, he had been told by his mother, did the spirits of the Divine Ones take on flesh and come back to Earth to live amongst the mortals.

This was very interesting!

While this being initially appeared male, like all of their kind, there was a balance of energies in his aura. That he had manifested on Earth was a sign, something his mother had often spoken of in hushed and reverent tones during her more lucid moments.

It meant that the end times were now upon them.

Roan had to know more about this hallowed being, so he watched carefully as the party debarked the ship together, lugging their personal belongings with them while a dockhand trundled a trunk with axe marks in the lid and side. They were detained and briefed for a while by dock authorities and the trunk searched before they were allowed aboard a paddlewheel ferry that would take them to the mainland docks.

Roan was torn between watching the unloading of the Solstice and following the ferry, but eventually his curiosity got the better of him.

He dove from the cliff and swam in. Bobbing up beneath the much smaller passenger dock on the jetty, he listened to conversations and salutations above as the ladies were helped off. The Numen leapt down without assistance, and was soon tripping lightly along the planks, chattering away with his more taciturn companions.

Roan watched them go until he saw the seal guns in the hands of the dock patrols, who were watching a small boat rowing off with a burly man and an angry, cursing woman wrapped in a cloak inside. It was time to go find Free, and see what she had learned. He would come back again under the cover of darkness, and perhaps search the town for them later.

He swallowed a lung full of air and dove deep, not coming up again until he was safely out of range of the gunners on the docks, and then swam out quickly, clicking and calling for his dolphin companion.

New Brooklyn Harbor

"We'll need to find a place to stay for the night before he disappears on us," Zephirine Merriwether commented as she strode along the rough and buckled shoreline dock with Aleta Kalama struggling to stay at her side. Zephirine was far taller and longer of leg, and she tended to be a bundle of energy on days when she wasn't actively using her wind calling talents. Aleta just always felt tired, for her fires came from within and that took a toll on her body that seemed to leave her perpetually hungry and fatigued.

"Agreed, but I don't much care where he goes. I could really use some rest," she said in a voice that sounded weary.

"I'm tired too, but he never seems to notice." The leather and wool clad woman frowned as she carelessly tossed back cascading brunette waves. The wind that always seemed to play around Zephirine had been pushing her along and tendrils of her hair were continually in her mouth or drifting across her hazel eyes. She inclined her chin ahead, toward the sprightly stepping man with his blonde mop bobbing above a rather outlandish and form fitting outfit of oiled leather and dark lace.

"I'd say he's forgotten all about us! We should get rooms and unpack before he heads out to the waterfront dives," she commented with distaste.

"Jordyn is not much for imbibing," Aleta answered rather breathlessly. The slender woman's dusky brow was furrowed and her gently backlit dark eyes flicked first this way and that, glancing around at the ramshackle coastal community that loomed ahead. The wind off the water was raw so she pulled her dull red cloak tighter around her compactly lithe form. "I don't know if he plans on shagging that one, but he does love to eat and chat, so we may not see him for a while, if and when he does go out for the evening. We should just find our own place, though I'm afraid I don't have much coin on me."

"I have plenty of trade goods," her taller companion reassured her. "I'll find us something decent. Oh but I'm not being considerate either, always getting ahead of you." Zephirine Merriwether stood almost a head higher than the small, dark skinned woman pacing beside her. She shortened her usual long-legged stride and slowed down to accommodate Aleta Kalama's winded scurry to keep up.

"Thanks, I'm just bone-tired today. A long rest in a real bed that doesn't smell like old fish would do me some good," Aleta said with a quick smile.

They were both a bit miffed at their flamboyant mentor, Jordyn Orion. He had been having an animated conversation with an amiable young man hauling Zephirine's trunk along with their other meager belongings, trundling it down the docks in some sort of wheeled contraption. He'd obviously forgotten all about his female companions for the time being. A skilled tale spinner, Jordyn's voice had varied between a high pitched bubble of excitement and a low toned, sonorous, conspiratorial murmur as he explained all they'd been through to the captivated youth. He gestured expansively as he wooed the shantytown young man with the adventurous highlights of their sea journey, one arm around his shoulders and his head tipped toward the rugged lad's ear.

"Do you think he actually is… propositioning him?" Zephirine said with a raised eyebrow. She didn't really care what Jordyn did in his spare time or with whom, but he was being rather flagrant about it, and that was terribly tacky.

"Most likely," Aleta said with scathing little laugh. It wouldn't be the first time her erstwhile tutor had found himself a dalliance along the way. He tended to be rather fickle and shallow in his torrid little romances, and she knew enough about him now to recognize the cockiness of his attitude meant he thought he was making another conquest. Something about his continually lascivious attitude was always rather disturbing, but she supposed after bouncing around the universe as a ball of energy for eons, a body would develop more than one voracious hunger that needed satisfying.

"He could at least wait until we get on dry land again," Zephirine grumbled as they turned a corner of the dock and headed down a boardwalk, away from the boat slips and toward the rough and tumble town of Yorkville looming in the distance. She ran on ahead, not waiting for an answer, for after poorly negotiating the sharp turn, the thoroughly distracted lad was struggling to get the trunk back onto the cart. He managed to tip it sideways and since the lock no longer worked after having been forced open by pirates at sea, Zephirine's things dumped all over the filthy, fish-stinking walkway.

"You've got to be more careful! Some of this stuff is very old," she admonished the young man, as he began unceremoniously tossing things back into the trunk. She pushed his hands away to reach into the depths and shoving other things aside, snatched up a bundle wrapped in a ratty shawl. Unwinding it quickly, she exposed a brass case about the size of the old world atlas the late Captain Jameson had kept in his quarters aboard *Solstice*. On the top side of the case was an antique gold sculptural detail depicting some sort of sea god or monster with black gemstone eyes, multiple arms, tendrils of hair, and a long serpent tail. It was still securely shut, but she pressed the eyes with two fingers and the case popped open.

"What is that?" asked Aleta. She had caught up and now came closer to help reload the trunk, but stood fascinated by the metal box in her companion's hands.

"What's left of an ancestor's orrery, a type of astrolabe. It's a family heirloom," Zephirine answered reverently, stroking the various components with a long forefinger. Inside, carefully packed into padded hollows of some very old velvet flocking of a rich, deep blue, was a set of gears made of a smooth silvery metal that shone with many iridescent colors, along with what looked like angled arms, springs, and a golden ball nestled in their respective niches. A large, half-round shaped area was empty.

"Something's missing here, should we look for it?" Aleta said nervously, for she had never seen anything so fine. She had no idea what an astrolabe did, but it was the kind of thing that in barter could buy a person room and board for a few cycles.

"No, that's been gone forever, and it's the reason I wanted to come to Columbiana in the first place," the other woman explained in a half-distracted manner. "I purposely took the job on the Solstice because it docks in New Brooklyn. There used to be a place here where such old things were once kept for the public to see. I thought with the city in ruins, I could go looking for it, but I didn't expect most of the buildings to be underwater!" Zephirine didn't pass along the fact that the base of the orrery had been purposely separated ages ago, to keep its powers from being abused, because that was something she had been told a Merriwether just didn't share with the rest of the world.

"I'd appreciate it if you wouldn't talk about seeing this—especially to Jordyn," she told Aleta. "People might want to steal it," she added in a low tone. Since the contents appeared to still be in pristine shape, Zephirine quickly refastened the cover and deftly wrapped the shawl back around it to end any further queries. Tucking it under her arm, she ran lightly off toward the much abashed lad as he wheeled her now upright and hastily repacked trunk along the boardwalk again.

Aleta watched her go, mystified as to her companion's sudden secretiveness, and then walked back to where Jordyn was standing like a statue, facing away from them. He had not even noticed the near calamity. Their mentor had inexplicably halted in mid-stride and turned to peer behind him, shading his aquamarine eyes against the setting sun's glare below the ever roiling clouds. He hadn't reacted at all when a grumbling and frustrated Zephirine brushed by him rather abruptly, or when Aleta walked back his way.

"I thought you said we need to stick together and keep watch over our things?" the smaller woman quipped drily as she stepped up beside Jordyn, who had now dropped well behind the hauler of their luggage to stop and stare out over the water.

"Don't you feel it?" he asked her in a distracted voice.

"Feel what?" she said curiously, with just a bit of apprehension.

"There's something out there," he said vaguely, and tipped his head like a dog listening for a command.

"What kind of thing?" Aleta asked with a bit of dread as her brown skin took on a soft sunset glow of its own. "Is it something bad?" She scanned out over the water too, but she couldn't see anything particularly threatening. Not much moved other than a few wheeling gulls and a small rowboat pulling away. Jordyn wasn't looking in that direction though.

"Well there are all sorts of things out there, and some of them are downright dangerous," Jordyn answered with a shrug. "But this one was simply curious about us, and it came up close for a bit, but when I turned to look for it, it swam off," he answered in a matter-of-fact tone, as if that explained everything.

"It's not one of those fish people, some sea monster, or a pirate, is it?" Aleta said with a worried sound in her voice as small front teeth nibbled away at a lip. She was hoping to get through at least a few days without another battle with someone or some *thing* determined to kill them.

"Noooooo...," Jordyn said quietly, his eyes narrowed to a speculative glance as he tried to read the aura of whatever had been trying to read his. "It's definitely not an Atlantean—that I'm certain of. As slimy as they are, the Atlanteans have a particular energy signature one can't mistake, if you know what I mean. Which you wouldn't of course," he said with a quick, lopsided smile to her confused look. "It's of humanoid size and shape, but not entirely human, though it's also nothing monstrous, or even threatening in any way. And while the pirate queen still lives, she's no threat to anyone right now."

"So what is it then?" Aleta asked softly so as not to be overheard. She had learned that there were many things in this world she'd had no idea actually existed before meeting Jordyn Orion, and most of them were far from friendly.

Jordyn stopped to think for a moment more before he spoke again. "I believe that this is one of the Atlantean's ancient Earthbound adversaries. Nothing to worry about really. The Finfolk are basically harmless to humans, unless you're a pretty little maid or a strapping young buck, that is," he added with a wink, before he took her arm and led her back down the dock and onto the boardwalk, walking quickly to catch up with their companions.

"So this… thing out there, it's someone you know?" Aleta asked uncertainly as she stumbled along beside him, hurrying to match his rapid gait as he propelled her down the uneven planks of the curving walkway above the rough and rocky shoreline.

"Oh no, we haven't met just yet," Jordyn said with a rueful shake of his head. "But I expect we will at some point. In fact, I'm rather eager to get to meet this anomaly. I think he or she–"

With that, his hand dipped into his shirt and pulled out the glowing Eye of Providence, his orb essence of power, and peered into its depths a moment. "Most definitely male, almost provocatively so. Yes, I believe we will be making his acquaintance soon enough." Jordyn was fairly shaking with excitement as he tucked the now softly glowing ball away.

Wonderful—another surprise guest. All Aleta wanted was a hot bath, a good meal, and a warm bed for the night, with no complications. "Shouldn't we catch up with Zee and get a place to stay?" she said in a wheedling tone. "She said she could pay for us all, and I'm hungry and could use a wash."

Jordyn laughed and patted her small behind affectionately before she shoved his hand away. "Of course dear. We'll pamper you properly and attend to your every need. After all, we are local heroes now, so there's no hurry and no worries. I sent our young friend on ahead with our things and told him to secure lodgings for us. It seems we're not going to have any trouble finding a place to stay, for we're now the toast of the coast, so to speak."

"Good, because I'm about worn out with all these so-called 'heroics'. I just want a few days of rest," Aleta answered petulantly, but Jordyn wasn't listening. The entire time he was talking to her, he never met her eyes, but kept watch over her shoulder out to sea. Something was moving about the pile of rocks and sand across the water, and it stood up on two legs and stared back at him. He could feel that intense gaze boring into his back even after he turned the corner and started walking resolutely toward the town ahead.

He'll come snooping around looking for us, and I'll make sure he finds us too!

~

Later that evening, after a long soak in a large steaming tub and plenty of scrubbing with long bristle brushes, both Aleta and Zephirine felt clean again at last. Hair shining and plaited or wound into a bun, and dressed in fresh clothing, they sat at dinner in a small dockside pub with Jordyn as he regaled whoever would listen long enough with tales of their adventures.

He had refused to finish any drinks bought for him, saying he had no tolerance for the stuff; though if truth be told, Jordyn could indulge all night without any ill physical effect. If he had taken any more than the occasional sip of alcohol in his corporeal human form, what would have become too very obvious was that Jordyn Orion had other forms besides the one they saw him in. With all inhibitions gone, the true nature of his being would be impossible to hold back, and that would be far too much of a shock for any mortal to comprehend. No one but another one of the ascended would have understood the tight rein Jordyn Orion had to keep over his physical world manifestation. He planned on keeping it that way too. The less who knew exactly who and what he was, the better.

Jordyn did nothing to discourage rounds consumed in his name though, as all evening long, the locals toasted his health and well being. What he learned from the tongues loosened by strong liquor and jovial camaraderie told him more about the area than his local hosts ever intended.

"This is quite an interesting place," he said to Aleta and Zephirine during one of his infrequent stops back at their table. "It seems to be run by some sort of local cartel that everyone tithes to. I suppose without an organized form of national government, that sort of thing would be likely to happen."

"Gang rule," Zephirine said with a sniff of disdain, as she looked around the room. "Common enough in the ports, where most of the commerce is based. We have them back in the Unified Islands too. A bunch of thugs they are."

I'll make sure he finds us too!

"We had warlords that controlled entire areas back home," Aleta interjected. "They got to decide who could scavenge or gather food, and where. They always took the best for themselves. No one mourned their loss when the war mechs took them out."

"So you're saying this is not a desirable turn of events?" Jordyn postulated, with a thoughtful look on his face.

"Certainly not!" Zephirine said indignantly. "These people have been through enough with all the wars and the flooding. The last thing they need is some despot setting himself up to rob them of what little they do have."

"And then these would-be robber barons fight amongst themselves, and innocent people get caught in the middle," Aleta added.

"And so what would you suggest in its place?" Jordyn asked pointedly. "From what I've heard, this particular despot of theirs keeps the pirates out to sea. Surely that is some benefit to the people here."

"Jordyn, I doubt those pirates stay away just because there are a few gunners on the docks," Aleta said with a frown. "The ones we fought had cannons and an airship. They could overrun this place in no time. There has to be some other reason the people here stay protected—something we don't know about yet." Aleta was thinking about another harbor area that had made a pact with the local demons out of desperation, and how stunned the people were to have been given their freedom when she and Jordyn had all but vanquished their erstwhile demonic overlords.

"And if these people in command here have some secret, it's likely something the common folk wouldn't understand the significance of," Zephirine added. "That makes them easier to exploit."

"I suspect you're absolutely correct on all of that, but I mean to find out for sure," Jordyn said and his eyes got that faraway look that said he was not telling all he knew. "And I know just whom to ask." He leapt to his feet and wandered off, seemingly lost in his own thoughts.

Aleta watched him walk away with troubled eyes. "He told me there was something out there, across the water, and it was watching us."

Zephirine sighed and picked up her eating utensil. "I suppose there will always be something we need to worry about. I just wish he would trust us more."

They finished their dinner in silence, wondering what dangerous adventures might lay ahead.

~

The night was dark when the young man took a walk down by the warehouse district. He had no doubt she'd find him. Everybody knew he'd talked to the newcomers first off, though he'd played stupid with them all.

"You looking for me, Willy Boy?" The woman's deep and throaty voice came from behind him, and the young man stopped where he was, his hands out to the side, showing he was unarmed.

"Yeah, figured I'd find you somewhere out here, Vixy," he said without bothering to turn around. She was a dangerous woman, but if she wanted to kill him, she'd have done it by now. He pulled a hand rolled cig from a leather case, and offered her one, passing it back over one shoulder. "I got some news for you."

"Do tell," the woman said as she took the proffered case. A match hissed as she lit up. She passed the sputtering stick and case back to him, and he lit his own casket tack before tucking the rest away and dropping the burnt match into the grit below, grinding it out with a booted toe.

He blew out a cloud of smoke that wreathed his head. "Them new people that come in today on *Solstice*, I trundled their trunk ashore. They're rich," he said it slowly, in a low voice full of suggestion.

"They got something I might be interested in?" she said in a breathless whisper meant for only his ears.

"I tipped over the trunk, to see what was in there. Lotsa fancy clothes and shoes, and a bit of old-timey silver plate, nothing too exciting. But the tall lady had a case with some shining bits and gears in it. One piece looked like solid gold. She said it was…" he had to think for a moment, "an orree, or something like that. It's a navigation device, c'ept the base was missing. The rest is s'posed to be here in the old city somewhere."

She snorted, blowing out smoke, and gave it careful consideration. She should tell the boss, but gold was hard to come by, and traded extremely high. "Whatever hasn't been pinched already is likely under water," she said slowly, "So no point in sharing that info. The gold and metal is worth something, but if we can get the whole thing together, it'd be worth a whole lot more. Just you and me know this?"

He grinned in the dark. Willy Tell was no doper, and he didn't flap his gums in the pubs like some of the others. "Other than the three as come ashore, yep. Just you and me."

"Let's keep it that way," she said quietly, and handed him a creased credit slip for his trouble. "Now don't you go get yourself drunk and yack this all over town. I need time to get to know these people, and figure out where the other part is. If His Highness gets wind of it, we'll never see any profit. Find out where they're stayin', and I'll be in touch."

She slipped off into the night as he was tucking the well worn credit slip into his shirt. He already knew where the ladies were staying, but wasn't going to let on yet, in case she might be willing to pay for that info too.

I'm for having another look at that thing anyways!

~

Jordyn slipped out of the pub sometime late in the evening, trusting that Aleta and Zephirine could see themselves back to their adjoining rooms. Both women were more than capable to make it home on their own, though they would likely be escorted anyway. David Shepherd had just come striding in with a new member of his crew, looking for "Missy Zee". Jordyn gave him a wink and a nod in their direction on the way out, but then scooted past without a word.

He managed to meld unseen into the shadows of the gloom of night and wandered alone down by the docks, expecting that someone or something else would come looking for him. Aquamarine eyes scanned the rippled surface of the sea from atop the rubble of a drowned building, where he sat and waited with arms wrapped around his knees for the curious being whom he knew would eventually come forth.

~

Aleta saw them coming first. She leaned in toward Zephirine, who was sipping some sort of drink made with hard cider and berries, and inclined her head.

"David is on his way over here, and he's got a friend with him," she said quietly.

"Damn!" Zephirine swore, setting down her drink. "Any chance we can slip off?"

"We'd have to go right past him, unless you want to try that piss-stinking back alley again," the smaller woman said with a sigh. They had already peeked out the rear exit once, and really didn't like the looks of the people watching them as they considered taking a shortcut across town to where their rooms were.

"No, I don't feel like beating anyone up tonight," Zephirine said in resignation. "Maybe he won't stay long."

"We'll find out in a moment," Aleta warned her, and then looked up with a resigned expression as the short and weathered man strolled over and set down two glasses of dark and foamy locally brewed beer.

After pleasantries were exchanged all around, and his hulking companion with mug in hand lumbered over to join them, the smaller man said with a lopsided grin, "I hope ye ladies twon't mind if me new mate Alfie and me join ye for a bit, jist te pass along some right good news." It was obvious from his reeking breath and bloodshot eyes that David Shepherd had already been celebrating for a few hours. "May I buy ye lovely lasses another round?" he added in a hopeful tone.

"Um, no thank you, we were just finishing up and getting ready to leave, because we're both pretty tired. But I suppose we can stay a bit longer and hear your good news," Zephirine said with forced cheerfulness. Aleta started to protest, but the other woman kicked her under the table, and she winced and went silent.

"Won't you sit down?" Zephirine continued with a tight smile, indicating the other two empty seats. She liked David, but he was a bit too forward for her, and tended to follow her around like a lost puppy. Still, it would not do to insult a potential future client. As it was, he hooked a chair with one foot and dragged it uncomfortably close, straddling it and raising his glass.

"Then I'd like to propose a toast. To me old Captain Jameson, may his restless soul be at peace beneath the waves. And to friends, lovers, and all past and future adventures," he added in his thick seaman's brogue. Before his hulking companion was actually seated, David downed a long swig before setting the glass down and wiping the back of a hand on his mouth.

Zephirine and Aleta raised half empty glasses and each took a polite sip, before they all thumped down on the table top. "Now what do we owe this pleasure to?" Zephirine said carefully, as Aleta's eyes flicked from one to the other of the men who had joined them. She wondered why Alfie was still standing, and why he kept scanning the room interior.

David Shepherd was beaming, and the beatific grin that split his grizzled face was infectious.

"Well, I jist got a commission to Captain of *Solstice* today. Seems as if I'm a bit o' what ye would call a 'folk hero' round these parts now, and the shipper company likes that. Makes the lesser pirates think twice afore they try and board ye, and even the long established ones don' like te tangle wit' a well armed ship and a canny captain. I get to pick me own crew an' all. Alfie here," he indicated the tall, heavy set man who had joined them, "is the first of that bunch."

He was ecstatic, and who could blame him? Both Aleta and Zephirine looked at each other, and then stood and congratulated him heartily, and all three were chattering away when Alfie finally broke in.

"Davey's got a proposition for ya," the other man said in a booming voice, his eyes locked on Aleta, so he didn't see his captain's glare for speaking out of turn.

"How about ye let me do the talking Alfie boy, aye?" the smaller man snapped.

"Go at it then, you were takin' long enough to get round to it." The girls sat down abruptly. Alfie was still standing.

"Will ye sit already?" Shepherd said, waving at a chair. "Ye makin' me nervous, hoverin' over me like me old Da."

Alfie was a large and burly seaman wearing a hand knitted toque, baggy trousers, and a shirt with the arms raggedly torn off, showing his big muscled biceps covered with tattoos. He had quaffed another long pull and banged his mug back down on the table again, standing with crossed arms while eyeing Aleta up and down in far too frank appraisal. The big man was rather intimidating looking, and somewhat loud, but his smile seemed lopsided and sort of vacant as he sat heavily into a chair and tipped it back against the wall, his long legs sprawled out beneath and propped up against the trestle table's spreader bar. Aleta couldn't tell if he was simple or just had too much to drink that evening, because though he never said much, that foolish smile never left his face the entire time.

"So tell us," said Zephirine cautiously, "What is this 'proposition'?"

"Might as well, seein' as Alfie 'ere let the cat out o' the bag already," Shepherd grumbled, but he crossed his arms on the back of the chair and leaned into it. "Well, I wanted this to be more social like, but since me loudmouth new chum 'ere spilled his guts, I'd like to ask ye both to stay on and ship back wit' us. When our rigging is done, the port side is repaired, and the hold is full, we'll be needing the help of a sail settler to guide us on the best winds back to the Unified Islands. Can't pay ye a lot, but there'll be steady work, and for certain a place for Missy Aleta too. The cookie needs help, and we can always use someone who can do washing and such. It's not a glamorous position, but *Solstice* can use all the good help and defenders she can get, and ye ladies be capable o' that and more..." Shepherd's voice drifted off as he took another healthy guzzle and set the empty glass down, reaching for the other.

Aleta shook her head but then looked aghast at Zephirine, who actually appeared to be considering the situation. "You're not thinking of abandoning Jordyn, are you?" she said in a worried tone.

"No, I couldn't do that," Zephirine said in a tight lipped reply, for how could she explain the inner voice of guidance? They'd think her daft if she said that a wind god she met in her unconscious state during their firefight with pirates on *Solstice* was refusing to let her leave Orion's side. She touched the winged silver pentacle amulet at her neck for reassurance that it had all happened that way and turned apologetic eyes on the man.

"Don't get me wrong Davey, it's an honor and a tempting offer, but I've promised Jordyn I'd join his team and I can't go back on that." She gave Shepherd one of her sweetest smiles and he returned a rueful grin, lifting his half empty glass in a salute.

"Well, I'm sorry to lose ye, but I'd expect no less from ye ladies. I hope Orion understands what a pair of treasures he has." He did look rather despondent as he drained his glass and stood up. "We be shipping out in two days and I'll be needed down at the boatyard bright and early, so we should call it a night as well. I guess this be goodbye."

He stood up, as perpetually smiling Alfie looked from one to another of them. Zephirine stood too. She also wanted to head back to their rooms, and while she and Aleta were perfectly capable of making their way safely through the gaslit streets, she didn't want to just abruptly dismiss David Shepherd. Besides the fact that one never knew when she would need a position to tide herself over a while, he was a friend and had basically saved her life when she had succumbed to battle fatigue, despairing she would never see the shore again.

"We're both still very tired and should turn in," she said, sweeping a hand out toward Aleta, who was also just getting to her feet, "And being strangers in Yorkville, we wouldn't mind if you'd walk us back to our flat. We've got rooms across town, but it's a somewhat of a hike there, and not all the neighborhoods here look friendly." She gave him a bit of a helpless look, appealing to his sense of gallantry. In all honesty it was a ploy to afford her and Aleta a quiet walk back without having to deal with local toughs, who would have no idea these female newcomers could very well take care of themselves.

"Alfie, on yer feet lad, we're about to escort two beautiful ladies home for the evening," Shepherd said, kicking the boot of his companion, who had been loathe to rise before he knew where they were off to. "We've barely been in port, but we have a heavy day on the morrow, with ship fitting and all. Let's square up with the barkeep, and head on our way."

∾

A half hour later the two women, accompanied by their male escorts, headed out into the night. There was nothing remarkable about that, except that one of them was a very tall, broad shouldered man who owed a certain waterfront crime boss some consideration for the money and opportunity he had been offered, and that powerful man did not take 'no' for an answer. As of yet, nothing concrete had come of such a lucrative overture, and now word had gotten around that this very foolish person was shipping out in a few days. The man in charge was about to rectify that situation.

There was no way this Alfred Noble character was going out to sea without first coming across with the goods and services he had been instructed to provide. If a lengthy 'talking to' with blunt force bodily harm didn't convince him of the error of his ways, he would wind up out at sea after all, albeit deep down into it, with rocks tied to his legs to keep his headless body below where the sharks prowling New Brooklyn Harbor would find him easily enough. But not before he had been thoroughly questioned in that backroom way they had with needles, knives, and hot iron bars shoved into sensitive places that made the strongest man scream out his deepest secrets and beg to tell more. That was something the boss had impressed on his 'associates' before he sent them out looking for Alfie. He expected them to do some knockabout convincing, and then drag the man back to him to secure a timely delivery. If that didn't work, he'd have Alfie Noble's big dumb head on a stake outside of the Yorkville limits as a warning that those who don't take whatever deals they were tendered didn't live long enough afterward to regret it.

Three men, noted to be local toughs and enforcers-for-hire, rose shortly after the foursome left the pub. Leaving some coin and a token on the table that told the barkeep he was wiser to have seen nothing unusual that evening, they sauntered out into the night. One of them, obviously the leader, drew a long bladed knife and tested the edge against his thumb, before he sheathed it and pulled a handled garrote from his shirt. He spoke quietly to his companions as they armed themselves with lead loaded clubs and knuckledusters—the weapons of brutal but effective persuasion. Soon they were circling the four walkers, looking for an opportunity to take down the big man before they had to deal with the pithy and well armed sailor, and the two women who would only get in the way.

Sons of the Sea

Jordyn had slipped into a semi-resting state, hunkered down in a seated position with his arms circling his drawn up knees, and chin resting on top. His unruly blonde mop of hair covered his face half the time, teased continually in the night's land breeze blowing out to sea. From a distance he appeared to be asleep, but his eyes were open, his hearing acute, and even his sense of smell accentuated.

Besides the perpetual waterfront stench of salt, rust, fish and decaying seaweed, there were wood smoke, burning dung, and tar scents coming off the land. None of that could cover the distinctive aroma of those things that inhabited the area—not for an ascended star traveler anyway. He could selectively choose to perceive whatever he focused on, and this night he was concentrating on the warm selkie-like musk of the gradually approaching swimmer.

Jordyn could feel the other presence trying to read him as it crossed the bay. After he had chosen his lonely spot to use as a neutral meeting place, he had sent out pheromones of attraction, knowing that the prevailing winds would carry them over to where the sea-being made his home. The response was almost instantaneous. There was a lot of curiosity and more than a bit of trepidation as the summoned one approached.

Carefully withdrawing the Eye of Providence from his shirt, Jordyn held it in both hands as the swimmer drew near. The Eye functioned both as an instrument of analysis and a bright beacon, for the last scion of House Orion wanted very much to be seen by this equally interested individual from the myths of old.

The swimmer paused briefly and clung to the waterlogged structure, looking upward through the last few feet of water. Jordyn didn't move a muscle, watching with a satisfied smile as the summoned one circled the base of the drowned building he sat atop. A head bobbed above the surface, and brown eyes in a faintly freckled face stared up into aquamarine ones that shone out brightly in the pale combined light of a waning gibbous moon glowing behind the ever present cloud cover and the Eye at a lowered phase. That was when Jordyn beckoned with his free hand, and got an answering wave.

Slow and cautious, the sleek, trim, and entirely naked male figure emerged dripping from the water. He deftly clambered up the wet, ruined side of the building to where the beaming starman was watching him with a calculating and appraising gaze. The building had no more than three floors left above the level of the sea, so eventually the mottled form crouched atop the farthest edge of the tilted, buckled top, watching warily as Jordyn Orion lifted the gently glowing Eye of Providence before him and scanned his aura from head to toe.

A half blood! That explained the strange energy signature that was not quite human, and barely selkie. Jordyn studied the wary figure with great interest.

So we already have a Finnman in this age too, as well as a Windmage and a Firecaller. Three of the four elementals located in such a short period of time! The Apocalypse approaches more rapidly than I thought. Now I only need to find my fourth team member and perhaps then we will have enough opportunity and the resources to gather the rest of the family treasures before the Apocalypsians raise a united army and force the End Times upon us.

"What does a Numen want from me?" queried the half-selkie, in a voice that was low and rather hoarse from not having been used in a while. His eyes watched Jordyn closely with a mixture of wonder and mistrust.

"Now that's a term I haven't heard used in ages. A title fit for those who were far more talented and well prepared than I am." Jordyn smiled in satisfaction, and tucked the orb away, before springing lightly to his feet.

The Finnman tensed, and his eyes never left the demigod before him.

"Oh yes, what *do* I want from you?" Jordyn went on, gesturing expansively as if confused, before continuing. "Well, to tell the truth, I haven't the foggiest idea," he answered himself, with hands braced on slim hips and shaggy head tipped sideways. "At least not yet, though I am sure you'll come in handy at some point. There may not be much you can do for us initially, though I'm sure you'll prove quite useful in the long run.

"But I suppose I should introduce myself first, before asking anything of you. I am Jordyn Orion of House Orion, which is the ancestral realm of my family. That would be way up there," he pointed with a dark leather gloved finger up toward the mostly invisible heavens. "Though I suppose that wouldn't make much sense to you, so we'll not discuss it further for now. Let us just say I came down here to help protect your perfectly wretched little world from those who would rape it of autonomy and throw the bones back to the Gods of War again. And you, my good fellow, can help me change all that," he added in a wheedling tone as he began to move forward toward the wary male before him, who looked as if he was ready to bolt, "if you join our cause."

The half-selkie didn't answer immediately, but those melting brown eyes looked up toward the cloud covered night sky, and then back at the slightly glowing being before him. "You have the wrong idea about me. I am no warrior," he said at last, standing up and preparing to back flip off the building, out into the water far below.

"Oh, but I think you are very much a fighter. You just don't realize your potential yet," Jordyn insisted. He had stopped moving forward but continued carefully assessing the Finnman. "I'll admit you're a bit thin and worse for wear. Not eating too well from the looks of it. Well, we can fix that right away," he added in a kind tone, for the scars of battles with other sea creatures, as well as those gained from encounters with some of the local humans he stole food from, were visible in the fine fur that covered the Finnman's body.

At the mention of food, Jordyn got the reaction he was hoping for. The brown eyes lit up and a very audible gurgle came from his midsection as the Finnman came forward a few steps. "I assume you must have a name also. Something you call yourself?"

"My name... my name is Roan," the Finnman said simply, looking down at his feet. "That's what my mother called me anyway."

"I take it she was the human parent?" When he got an affirmative nod, Jordyn continued, "And sadly, no longer on this side of life's veil." He stated that gently, noting the drooping of Roan's head at her mention. Jordyn began to move closer, walking around him now, admiring his sleek and plush coat. He was young and rather thin, but superbly fit and in excellent health.

"If you mean is she is dead, then yes," Roan said with a sigh. "At least ten cycles I've been on my own. I never knew my Da. He left her before I was born, and we moved around a lot. The people called me a monster and they shunned mother," he explained, spreading his partially webbed fingers, and then running them down his sides. "It was a hard life for her, and then she got so very sick." The memories he had seldom spoken of moistened Roan's eyes, and left wet trails in the fine plush of his cheeks.

"You're not a monster my boy. You're the answer to a lot of prayers," Jordyn reassured him quietly, and he put his arm around Roan's shoulder, almost thrilling at the feeling of wiry coiled muscles beneath the mottled fur. "And you're also not alone anymore, because I'm going to make you part of our little family of adventurers."

They talked for a while longer atop that abandoned old high rise building that was mostly underwater, until the tide changed, and tiny glimmers of hidden sunrise streaked the eastern horizon.

~

Alfie Noble was a bulky man, with a normally affable yet closed-mouth personality, but he had plenty of street smarts and could give a fine accounting of himself in a fair fight. He was not just big, but muscular too, as he'd worked the docks since he was old enough to lift a crate by himself. This fight was not going to be fair at all, and he knew that. He just hoped these pugs trailing them waited until the girls were safely inside and Shepherd had tromped off to his own flat before they tried to take him down.

Alfie had been aware that they were being followed before they left the gaslights of the downtown area behind. There were multiple men ranging around them, likely armed and not averse to jumping a bloke from behind and staving a bloke's head in with a blunt object. He also knew who sent them.

It had taken steel cullions to refuse an offer from local mob boss Georgie Rushman, because one way or another, the powerful man with the long reach controlled a good part of the waterfront. He expected and generally gained full cooperation, for his reputation as someone who didn't take no for an answer had left more than one would-be 'business associate' who didn't comply with a directive, dropped headless into the bay. What Rushman wanted in this case was Alfie's skill in designing large explosions that would go off reliably underwater, and made no secret of the fact that this was just the first of several requests that would be forthcoming. Alfie was to deliver both the device and the instructions for assembling and arming it, in the event of his untimely demise if it failed.

That was a secret formula the son of a shipbuilder and a naval demolitions expert was not willing to share, because it would bring far too much instability upon their area and likely result in martial law again. The livelihood of his friends and neighbors depended upon the local economy remaining stable and safe, and no one wanted the pseudo-government of Columbiana taking too hard a look into their business. To have some treasure hunting kingpin blowing up half the harbor wasn't going to help that. More importantly, disturbing the old green lady under the waves was not going to turn out well for anyone—not if what slept beneath her skirts and protected the harbor from being overrun by the merfolk and pirates was taken out. But then again, that blowhard Georgie Rushman had never seen those murdering invaders of the deeper water up close. Alfie had fought both, as had his well-traveled mother, and he knew they were far more of a threat to the community than the local gang boss and his downtown bullies ever imagined being.

So as he walked the silent and echoing streets escorting Captain Davey's lady friends back to their rooms, Alfie kept a careful watch around them. Initially Rushman's hired thugs just shadowed him, but did not move in closer, likely not wanting too many witnesses. That could mean they intended to take him alive, and torture the location of the formula from him. Well, they'd have to read his mind for that, because it was never written down but created to fit the need, and each device was like a piece of original art.

He fidgeted a bit while waiting for Shepherd to say his slurred goodnights to the tall and cool-mannered brunette looker, hoping the captain got his kiss and would be gone before the fight came to them. As the toughs began to close in, the big man just stood there whistling a merry tune with his hands thrust deep in his pockets. He was uneasy about the odds, but he always kept a few secrets hidden—items only a Noble would know how to manufacture and use.

~

All through their stroll across town to walk Orion's ladies to their flat, David Shepherd had noted his male companion's uneasiness. Even as inebriated as he had been, the experienced seaman had been in his share of brawls and scuffles, and so he recognized the wariness of a hunted man. Alfie wasn't much of a talker for a reason and that was because he had something to hide. That 'something' was liable to erupt at any point, judging by the sound of quiet footfalls that ambled along behind and around them like stalking cats. Best they get Missies Zee and Aleta safely indoors for the night before the rumble started.

It hadn't bothered Shepherd to hire a man with a past. Many of those he had sailed with over the cycles were running from one thing or another, and he'd learned not to ask nosy questions. Still, judging from the larger man's level of alertness and concern, this was something far more serious than a lover's jealous mate or a gambling debt left unpaid. Alfie was expecting to fight for his life, and the new captain of *Solstice* assumed he would be pulled into that brouhaha along with him. Well so be it; never let it be said that Davey Shepherd left one of his crewmen high and dry.

They dropped the two women at the bottom of the outdoor stairwell of their rooming house, and after a lingering goodnight, he made sure they were safely climbing up before leaving. With the unspoken communication of a couple of experienced wharf rats, they nonchalantly began taking a different route back than the one they had come in on, heading the fight to an area where many dockhands and seamen roomed when in town, figuring on securing a bit of support. There was nothing necessary to say about what was ahead, just a mutual understanding between two men who had both grown up in the tough coastal waterfront areas of their respective homelands, and so understood the perpetual organized criminal elements those regions attracted. Since the long cycles of wars had grounded most air transport and taken out all but rudimentary communications, shipping was what had kept the scattered people left in the world in touch with one another. Whoever controlled a major port was the most powerful player in his or her part of that continent, and gangs of organized criminals were the norm in the more successful areas. New Brooklyn's harbor had that kind of status, and most of the sailors were tired of it.

Whoever these guys were, they wasted no time. Passing quickly behind the building where they had left the girls, both men could hear the stealthy footsteps approaching rapidly now. As the first of the heavies came at Alfie, David Shepherd drew his service blaster and took a bead on him. When the lead weighted tip of a blackjack hit him first on the wrist, and then on the temple, the shot went wild. He went down in a heap that the man accosting him leapt over to join the other two goons already engaged in working Alfie Noble over.

～

Aleta and Zephirine had just said their goodbyes, and were headed up the stairs to the outdoor landing where their second floor walk-up's door was, when a commotion broke out in the back alley. The two women looked at each other in consternation and they both sighed. This was one of those tense neighborhoods where no one wandered far outdoors in the night, and so the sounds of a fight could only mean one thing: David and Alfie were in trouble.

Suspicions had been prickling at Aleta's nerves since Shepherd and his wary and taciturn friend had shown up. Now with this noise of a fracas

...The shot went wild.

out back, it was enough to set her skin glowing. She paused on the rickety stairs below Zephirine as the taller woman turned back, and their eyes met.

Aleta shrugged her shoulders. "It might not be them, you know," she said quietly. She was tired and really wanted to get to bed.

"But you do know we were followed, don't you?" Zephirine insisted, jiggling the key attached to a lanyard draped over her wrist. "I could hear someone pacing us all the way from the pub. I just figured they didn't want to make a move toward you or me while the boys were around."

"Yes I did know, but I figured they were looking for a chance at us too. They must have been planning to get David and Alfie alone the entire time," Aleta said and she turned and hurried back down the stairs. "We'd better go bail them out of this one."

"I suppose. But damn it, but I've *got* to get inside and pee first," Zephirine said with a groan.

"Go! I'll check it out, and let you know what's happening," Aleta promised. "If you see me light up, come on down and join the party." In spite of the dark night in an unfamiliar area, the small woman had gained enough confidence in her fighting abilities that she had no qualms about facing a simple back alley brawl.

"I'll meet you out there in a few," Zephirine promised. She started back up the stairs, hustling the rest of the way up to their flat.

Neither of them saw the young man who hurried away beneath the fire escape from their rooms with an old shawl wrapped around something hard and metallic.

~

To Alfie Noble's credit, he was neither a coward nor a man who would willingly abandon a comrade who was vulnerable. He was certainly not going to run off and let his new captain take a brutal beating on his behalf. When he saw Shepherd go down, he fought his way free, tossed a couple of items that had been in his pocket, and then stood over the man, covering his ears and grinning like an idiot.

Unfortunately the small explosive devices he had thrown at the guys accosting him were not enough to do more than delay the inevitable, as they had expected as much from the man known to be a wizard at creating things that went '*bang*'. As bright and noisy as they were, they were easily dodged, and these pugs were far more afraid of incurring the boiling wrath of their employer than superficial skin burns or losing some hearing to a homemade flash bomb. While a wobbly Shepherd was slowly getting back on his feet, Alfie stepped between him and the two men who still came rushing at them, fists and clubs raised and ready to rumble.

Even with blood streaming down his face from a scalp wound, and double vision caused by a blow that had somehow not managed to entirely brain him, Alfred Noble gave a good accounting of himself that night. Still the men who came after him were ruthless and well prepared, and they knew how to read a mark. Two of the assailants beat Alfie backwards, and while the big man fought like a cornered animal, he was no match for these armed and ruthless professional intimidators. He was battered repeatedly, and slowly going down under a barrage of clubbing, punches, and kicks, though he still refused to give in. It all ended when the third goon grabbed a still groggy Davey Shepherd and dragged him around with an arm behind him, holding a long, shining knife at the smaller man's throat.

"Give it up, Noble," he said harshly, pressing the blade against Shepherd's neck, "Or I'll carve this two credit captain of yours a brand new smile."

"Cap'n has nothing to do with this," Noble insisted breathlessly.

"Big George don't care about that," the other man said as he deftly slipped a garrote from one hand to the one shifting the knife without taking his attention off the man he was holding. He could feel Shepherd's head and shoulders tensing for a head butt attempt and he dug the tip of the knife into his grizzled chin to remind him how sharp it was. "All the boss wants is his goods and services rendered. If you stall too long, that ship will likely need a new captain, because this one will be feeding sharks. That's what happens to the friends of those who don't do as they're asked in a timely manner." He nodded at the men holding a spitting mad and bloody Alfie Noble back, and the beating began in earnest.

Suddenly there was a great flaring of light that came at the edge of what was left of his vision as Alfie Noble caught a blow he couldn't ward off. Before he could make sense of it, he went limp in the arms of the men who were beating him, and the three of them fell into a pile on the trash-strewn ground.

Together We Stand!

Sneaking back into town late at night was not something Jordyn found particularly daunting. Once he had parted company with Roan on the top of the flooded building, the Finnman had simply jumped back into the gently lapping harbor waves and began heading for shore. Jordyn had once again dissolved his essence into the Eye of Providence and teleported back across the water. He landed on the dock where it met the boardwalk and waited for Roan to surface. He'd morphed his outfit at the same time into something he felt a bit more at home in. The Finnman had swum fairly rapidly, and pulled himself up the pilings until he could grasp the edge. Jordyn offered him a hand up.

"They'll know me here, and I'll get shot at," Roan warned Jordyn as he quickly scanned the area. The dock patrol was out of sight, but they had harassed him before and he was always wary.

"We'll just go inland a bit, and you'll be fine," Jordyn reassured him. "We've got to get you fed, and fix you up with a place to stay. Perhaps a bath and some clothing…" His voice trailed off as he headed in the opposite direction from the one that he had taken with Aleta and Zephirine earlier—out toward the seediest side of town.

The mention of clothing was somewhat troubling to Roan, who had been away from human society for so long. "You changed what you were wearing very quickly," he remarked. He had been in the water when the starman left and had not seen him go, so had no idea how it was even possible that Jordyn had already donned a brand new outfit.

Jordyn did not bother explaining. "Do you like it?" he said, preening like a young girl. "I could get you something like this if you want."

"It's alright I guess. I suppose I better find something to wear too, just not anything so… frilly," Roan said unhappily, looking down at himself. It had been many cycles since he'd bothered to think about clothing at all. It tended to get tattered and frayed with the constant exposure to sea water and rocks, and sometimes impeded his swimming. It really wasn't much help at all with the exposure either. His mother used to insist that no matter how raggedy his things became, he get dressed each day. Since her death he wasn't allowed into towns very often, so he had stopped wearing clothing altogether.

"Well, we will get to that in due time my boy," Jordyn said, steering him along the boardwalk toward the most poverty stricken part of town, "But first let's get you something to eat."

They wandered toward the lights of the downside of town together, a wet, naked, and lightly furry man with partially webbed fingers and toes and faintly mottled hide alongside the clown prince of the nighttime pubs. Besides his well teased hair and darkly lined aquamarine eyes, Jordyn was in one of his more outrageous outfits, with oceans of lace down the front and ringing the cuffs of a shirt worn under a dark high collared jacket over tightly laced leather leggings. He had headed them into the red light district, where outlandish was the norm, hoping to find an all night eatery with decent food and no bias against those with a rather abnormal appearance.

They walked for a while, avoiding the few people they met until they were out of sight of the harbor itself. As they approached the more inland area Jordyn had in mind, local hovels lined both sides of streets that still had some vestiges of the bombed out hulks and rusting iron skeletons of high rise buildings amongst them. Most of the usable material had been scavenged when Yorkville had risen from the ashes of a city that had never slept, until the wars and resultant radiation killed off most of the original occupants. This far inland, there was quite a mix of migrants from all over Columbiana, and so Jordyn and Roan were a bit less of an anomaly than they would have been closer to the waterfront.

"Ah, this looks promising," Jordyn commented brightly as they approached a side street where even after midnight, the neighborhood was boiling with activity.

"If you say so," Roan answered in a troubled voice, because with all the noise and lantern light, it felt like a trap to him, and he was longing for the open water again.

"Don't worry my boy, you'll fit right in," Jordyn reassured him as they started to move down that gaudy carnival of an avenue offering all of life's most prurient temptations.

～

Slipping around the side of their rooming house wasn't much of a feat for Aleta, as skulking figures passing through the area were not something anyone dared remark upon. Residents were expected to secure their own rooms, and the local constabulary paid homage to the whims of the real authorities, the roaming gang members, who wanted access to anyone they had business with at any time of the day or night. Consequently, there were no patrols in the area that evening, as the local watchman had been told to take a hike for a while. He was sitting in a bar on the other side of town getting progressively drunk, idly wondering who was going to get whacked tonight.

The watchman's position was just for show anyway. By dusk, the backstreets outside the entertainment district were quiet, as most honest folk tried never to be out after dark. To inadvertently witness something you shouldn't in Yorkville generally had you winding up as shark food, so the average citizen went on her or his way, ignoring the sounds of blaster fire or beatings, pretending not to notice the mutilated bodies that occasionally bobbed in the harbor the next morning. In exchange, they were a fairly prosperous lot who didn't have to worry about blockades or the coastal pirate ships with cannons that could reduce a settlement to rubble before pillaging and raping through the decimated town. So it was an equitable trade-off of sorts.

Aleta understood at least part of that, as Jordyn had told her that his enamored young acquaintance had related in a nervous whisper that the seal gunners on the docks were hired and equipped to keep the pirates and riffraff out to sea. That was why Yorkville residents had an uneasy truce with their local gang, so that the greater of both evils did not have to be dealt with. In the meantime the hard life of a ruined but rebuilding seaport area went on for most people, keeping them too busy to think about running their town without the iron fist of Big Georgie Rushman involved.

Making her way to the back alley proved to be more of a problem of layout than interference. The ramshackle construction of the entire waterfront area was built from old rubble and scavenged wood carted from the blasted out and flooded city that once had been a bustling metropolis of steel and stone. Most of the buildings in the immediate shoreline area were two stories high, with pawn shops, pubs, small stores, and lending houses on the bottom floor, and rooms to let above. The girls had chosen their current flat because the shop below was supposedly a laundry. It was run by a fierce looking old woman who preferred hand rolled smokes, and consorted with some rather nefarious characters. Men with bundles that did not look like wash under their arms and blasters tucked into belts came and went at odd hours, so they suspected the laundry was the minor part of the business. Their landlady had seen pleased enough to get the antique teapot and fancy clothing Zephirine had traded for their room and board, and she never bothered them afterward.

Upstairs and in the back was where their rooms were, and there were no windows facing the back alley or the one on the farther side, just a jump door at the end of the hall that led to a rickety fire escape serving both buildings. They used the more secure front stairs to get up and down, as the only other way in did not appear to be very safe.

The buildings around theirs leaned this way and that, their upper floors protruding over the streets and alleys, almost touching, making a tight squeeze through a dark, unlit passage filled with refuse and rats. Aleta was trying to get around the side of the building unseen. She didn't dare risk a light and warn the combatants of her coming, which is why when she finally made it out back, she had not expected to see an eight foot high wall of mortared rubble with some kind of twisted, rusting wire full of sharp edges strung along the jagged edge top.

"Damn, it's always something," she grumbled under her breath, hiking up her skirt before beginning to climb up. "Be a nice time to learn how to fly." The sounds of the altercation that came from the far side indicated someone was taking a real trouncing, as there were body blows, grunts, swearing, and the snarls of men engaged in close combat. "Why can't we pass through any area of this blasted world without having to play frigging heroes again?"

There were a couple of muffled small explosions on the other side that lit up the darkness. She pushed herself harder, frustrated over having to deal with that kind of situation in a long skirt. It snagged on the stones and interfered with her climbing, and in irritation, she wrapped it up around her waist as she neared the top. Peeking over, she could just make out men wrestling in the half gloom. The big person going down underneath the two figures pummeling him right below her had to be Alfie, and it was clearly Davey Shepherd who was being dragged to his feet across the alley, a long knife blade held by his assailant glinting in the dim glow of a distant gas light.

There was no time to lose!

Aleta ripped the skirt off, and clambered quickly to the top of the wall. Lighting up, she gave a blood curdling war cry as she jumped off, landing fully aflame on the back and shoulders of the man who was trying to turn Alfie's face into a pulpy mask of bloody seeping cuts and bruises.

The batterer howled and recoiled as the heat of her projecting flames burned through his clothing and singed his hair, and she hung on grimly as his body bucked and he reared up in pain and fear. Using the momentum of her attack, she latched on and rolled the man over and off Alfie before the heat reached down toward him too.

The burned man landed atop her, screaming and flailing, desperately trying to regain his feet as her flames licked over his exposed skin, scorching his hair and remaining clothing.

Aleta rolled over with him again and then glared down into his frightened eyes, her face a mask of pitiless contempt lined by firelight as she viciously kneed him in the groin. When he let go with a shriek of pain and terror, she pulled away, heaving to her feet gasping for breath, for his sudden weight had knocked the wind from her and she'd had to let the fires die down a bit to catch her breath.

This one assailant at least was no longer any threat; for he lay twitching and moaning, curled into a fetal position, clutching his smashed and burned genitalia. Alfie Noble lay nearby too, beaten almost senseless, his face a swollen mass of dark marks and blood, his breath coming in gurgling whines from lungs straining within cracked and bruised ribs.

Aleta wasted no time, but whipped around like a cat, looking for the others, her feral eyes blazing with anger. She was determined to make them all pay for what they had done to her friends. The man holding Shepherd had already scrambled away. The tiny woman with her body all aglow and fingers dancing with flames strode forward undeterred, her orange flickering eyes glaring at the third man, who had backed off already. He dropped his blackjack as she advanced on him but was fumbling awkwardly for a pocket laser with trembling fingers still thrust into brass knuckles.

"You're the next one who's going to get cooked, so I wouldn't try anything stupid," she warned him as she whipped flames outward to flare in his face, which blanched in horror and disbelief. He put his hands up as he continued to backpedal and stumbled over some trash, falling down on his rear end before leaping to his feet to turn tail and run. Her flames followed him as he pounded back down the long, dark back alley toward anywhere that fiery demon women didn't drop out of thin air.

"Who's... *next?*" Aleta asked with a snarl as she whirled back around. She advanced on the man holding the knife to a wide eyed David Shepherd's side while he yanked on the garrote that was now around the other man's throat.

"Back off you flaming little freak, and maybe he won't get hurt," the man said smoothly, obviously a pro who had seen mutants before. "You get too close, he gets his neck rung."

"You must want to be on my burn list too," she purred in low, throaty and feral tone as she advanced on him slowly, the glow around her flaring up like a corona and the golden blaze of anger flashing in her eyes. "I've torched entire ranks of demons to a crisp without a second thought," she added, thinking back on her previous battles with the undead, Atlantean mermen, and pirates. "What makes you think you'll survive this, you damn fool?"

"Because I've got him, and you'd have to take out both of us," the smirking man added as he increased his chokehold on a now barely breathing David Shepherd, who was struggling to keep the garrote from throttling him. His assailant dug the knife into the skin of his ribs a bit deeper, just to make sure Shepherd didn't try anything fancy with a head butt again. "I don't think you want him dying back here just because Alfie Noble is an idiot who doesn't know how to deal. You're all as good as dead anyway if you stay here any longer, because my boss isn't the forgiving type. He'll come back after anyone who touches one of his own or interferes in a bit of persuasion. So maybe you'd best get out of Yorkville now and forget about what you saw tonight. Otherwise a whole lot more people are going to get hurt."

He twisted the garrote ends for emphasis, and Shepherd's face turned blue as his eyes went wide and he began to flail and choke.

Aleta stopped her advance abruptly. She had no idea what to do next. If these men took Davey with them, he'd likely never see the light of day again. She knew she was out of her element now, because hostage negotiation was something Jordyn would have been better at.

Drat him for going out and leaving us alone again!

"Why don't you just let him go and take Alfie instead," she said with concern, figuring that at least she could stall for time, and maybe someone else would come along. "David has nothing to do with whatever trouble his friend is in."

The man gave her a triumphant look. "I don't think so sister. Noble's more likely to become useful to us if he knows he's got something to lose. You tell that big idiot when he wakes up that if he wants to see this sea rat captain of his again, he'd better show up by sundown with the device in hand. Now I'm going to walk out of here, and you're going to let me, or I'll see you all on the other side of hell."

He got to his feet dragging Shepherd with him, the smaller man not even squirming to get free. Instead he was trying to convince the man hauling him along that he was cooperating, hoping to get in a warning shout. Aleta was in real danger now and David Shepherd intended to at least die a hero.

The man who had run off had slipped back, and he was now holding David Shepherd's dropped service blaster in one shaking hand with a bead drawn on Aleta, as a couple more men of their acquaintance advanced. His captor had kept her talking so long, she didn't sense the other presences coming up behind her before a blaster bolt from a weapon set on KILL knocked her to the crackled pavement and she knew no more.

～

The first of the several swaggering figures in outrageous outfits and masks passed them by as they made their way along the rutted byway known locally as Down Sodom. Most people of that era didn't recall what the reference to an ancient realm meant, but Jordyn did. He found it rather humorous that the old Canaanite rebel king Bera and his precious little realm was still part of folk memory. Bera had been a rather likable chap, if a bit lax in keeping his licentious people under control. This outskirt part of Yorkville was actually quite reminiscent of that city of another era, for all the vices of humanity were represented there.

Gin mills, dance halls, brothels, flop houses, coca snuffing and opium smoking dens lined both sides of the street. The cheapest, most rat and roach infested, cracked walled rooms-to-let were upstairs, most of them occupied by the local prostitutes and their revolving clientele. Music and raucous laughter filled the air while men and some women stood huddled together in knots, talking quietly about deals they could or had made. Some slumped over or sat propped against buildings in a half stupor, while others squatted on the curb begging for a few coins or small trade items to get their next swig, 'bitty tin', or pipe full. A few sprawled in the alleys sleeping it off, or heaving their stomachs dry in the gutters. Now and then, someone dragged off the body of one who would never rise again. Gaslights that barely chased off the shadows revealed some quickly glimpsed carnal acts taking place behind overflowing refuse piles, and shadows in unlit corners hinted at even more lascivious behavior.

Female forms of all ages, racial mixtures, and in some cases genders, strutted around in relatively very little clothing on the rough board sidewalks, along with some very attentive pimps and potential clientele searching for fornication at a fee. Poor Roan didn't know where to look first, there were so many half naked women promenading past that he was overwhelmed. His selkie heritage quickly made itself known in becoming prominently aroused by all the fleshly debauchery around him. It wasn't long before others were noticing that too.

"Ahoy there Furball!" one woman called out stridently, "Want to give that rudder of your'n a good turn?" She and her friends laughed uproariously at Roan's discomfiture as he looked first down at himself, and then back to them with a half smile of surprise. Most of the women he desired had never been that easy to catch, and many times he had run from a town being chased by men with clubs and staves after getting too close to someone's wife or daughter. Yet these women were openly offering themselves to him, and while that was intriguing, he was very confused as to why.

"Not tonight ladies, he's with me," Jordyn said with his hand on Roan's shoulder, which for some reason made the local strumpets laugh all the harder. Jordyn stretched up to whisper in the taller Finnman's ear, "They charge for those kinds of services, and we've better things to do with the credits." He noted the sudden droop in Roan's posture and arousal level with some satisfaction.

"Oh," was all Roan said, for he had never been this far into any town before. "Too bad I didn't think to bring any fish to trade!"

Jordyn's giggles went on for a long time and Roan had no idea what was so funny about what he had said.

~

When Zephirine heard the muffled explosions and then Aleta's shrill war cry, she knew things had already taken an ugly turn. There was no time to run around front, so she climbed out gingerly onto the rickety fire escape's landing to get a better look at the situation. She couldn't see much from where she stood, but the light of Aleta's fires lit up the back alley and shone over a tall wall built of mortared rubble that appeared it would be hard to climb.

From the sound of things, the fight was ongoing, and she fretted that there was no easy way over there. She couldn't reach the ground without risking a broken limb, and then there was still the wall to climb. The joint fire escape that plunged between the buildings angled toward the front with no space between those stairs and the outer walls to crawl over and down. Its stairwell did not intersect with the front set, so she would have to run all the way back inside, out and down, and then around the far side of the building looking for access to that alley. And she still had to some-how get over that wall. It was too far to jump for it.

"Everything has to be so damnably impossible!" she groused.

She stood there transfixed for a moment with a breeze playing around her, noting that Aleta's discarded skirt was hanging off the wall and flut-tering like a cape. That gave her an idea.

The winds that she could gather around her had lifted many things. She had blown the bodies of her attackers well into the air before she let go and they crashed to the ground, and some of those people had been far heavier than she was. Perhaps she could ride the wind herself? She had never tried collecting them in one spot before, but theoretically, she should be able to maintain their support long enough to get her safely over that wall and down into that back alley where the action was.

Time was of the essence, for there were screams, shouts and a low voiced conversation that ended in a blaster report. Aleta's fire went out and the area became dark again.

Zephirine Merriwether clutched the pentacle pendant at her throat and whispered a prayer to her patron deity as she pulled a whirling cushion of air currents toward her, and stepped tentatively out onto their buoying mass.

Down, But Not Out!

Georgie Rushman was a big, stocky man and the chair he leaned back in creaked ominously beneath his bulk. With sandy brown hair now receded and gone gray, the former pit wrestler and street fighter had let himself go soft in the easy life his overbearing influence had bought him over the last dozen cycles. What was left of the muscles he had built in younger days slumped beneath pads of fat on arms, legs, neck, and belly. He still moved fast though, and always had a blaster at hand, a blade in one shoe, and a snub nosed telephase peashooter in a hidden holster.

Ever the target of unfriendly takeover attempts, Rushman had cheated death several times via a one-way protection field generator that allowed him to press the fist shaped head of a gold stickpin to key up an energy shield that could be broken only on the inside by an outgoing charge. He was cold-hearted and ruthless, and surrounded himself with loyal toughs whom he paid well with credits, dope, prostitutes, and favors. He had people killed just because he didn't trust them, or they had otherwise displeased him, including two ex-lovers. In his estimation, human beings were generally replaceable, as there were always plenty of others lining up who were willing to carry out his orders.

Rushman owned virtually the entire waterfront, and was spreading his organization's tentacles throughout the inland area. His reach was long, and his influence felt well outside the harbor town of Yorkville. His ultimate goal was to establish himself beyond the ocean as well, for having a presence in each port of call would make it easier to control the shipping companies that paid local homage to him. He would eventually buy up or put out of business those who didn't cooperate. He was a big man with big plans of creating a monopoly on docking, with first right of refusal on whatever goods were in the cargoes that moved through the ports.

To accomplish all that though, took funds and the influence to buy favors. Without a strong centralized government in Columbiana, credits were in short supply, and the barter of goods and services was the preferred exchange. Relentlessly Rushman searched for even more lucrative means of raising enough capital to finance the ambitious plans he had. His latest venture was selling artifacts.

The part of the city still above water had long since been looted and ransacked, stripped of everything portable, right down to the reusable building materials. But beneath the waves was a treasure trove of undiscovered wealth just waiting for someone to come and claim it. The problem was that the area was not easily accessible and was populated by large, hungry sharks; which made unprotected dives dangerous. The technology to reach those parts of buildings deep below sea level either no longer existed or was extremely expensive to produce, as most of the remaining engineering and manufacturing in Columbiana concentrated on war and defense materials. Many a man had died in the depths trying to get inside and out of the sunken wreckage with the prizes they held, and no more than a mere handful of items made it to the surface. But what Big Georgie Rushman had seen and heard about that was still hidden down there had whetted his desire to find a way to cash in on the fears of others and claim the booty left below as his own.

Yet even with the threat of painful death for refusing, he could no longer find divers willing to risk their lives. Besides the large and predatory sharks, there was the rumor that something large and demonic supposedly lurked well down within the darkened watery depths. Some called it a serpent, others a monster, but whatever it was, it kept even the threat of pirates and warships out of their vicinity for fear of incurring its wrath. It had not been seen above water in two generations, but now and then the ocean outside the bay, back where the old timers said the harbor had once ended, boiled as something huge and mysterious moved along beneath the waves before diving. Bodies that floated out to sea were tugged below, most often by sharks, but occasionally a huge webbed and clawed appendage would reach out of the water and snatch them away. Warning shots fired in its direction by the seal gunners on shore did not seem to faze it, and it was never at the surface for very long.

It had been said long ago that only the Lady of the Harbor had protected humanity from this curse, for she had been raised over a starry base on an island that kept the monster buried, and that as long as she remained standing, then New Brooklyn Harbor was safe. Now her island was submerged, and she laid broken apart deep beneath the waves. Never would a boat dare pass over the spot where she rested for fear of waking the wrath of the homeless beast, which guarded the sunken city for all eternity.

Initially Rushman welcomed the local superstitions, for though he personally scoffed at them, they kept the treasure hunters out of what he now considered his territory. Since it was also keeping him from accessing all sorts of untapped wealth, he had devised a plan for taking out whatever marine monstrosity lurked beneath the lapping waves. It was a plan that involved precisely set explosives targeted to blow up the remnants of the colossal icon that lay on its side and reportedly provided a home for the creature. Since most beasts went to lair when they were threatened, that was where they would hunt it.

The old maps that he had paid dearly for called the sunken area Liberty Isle, and the grand dame of Columbiana was rumored to rest in pieces on her side nearby, her barnacle encrusted skirts open to whatever took shelter beneath the waves. Once Rushman had the explosives he needed, his people would get down to work, and then the rest of the sunken treasures would be his to plunder.

And that was where Alfie Noble came in.

The night was getting on, and no reports. Rushman sat abruptly upright, impatient for results.

"Where's that damn fool Noble? I told them I want him in here pronto!" his voice barked in a rusty tenor, like a small dog with a pugnacious attitude.

"The boys will be bringing him in sometime tonight," the slightly smiling woman said smoothly, after she exhaled the smoke of one of his imported cigs from both nostrils. "Providing they don't blow it and let him escape again."

Uncrossing her long legs and sliding easily off the conference table where she had been studying maps and charts, she tossed strawberry blonde curls back before stalking across the floor like a hunting cat. Her lithe form encased in an urban camo catsuit of grays and olive greens, she glided in soft soled boots to a window covered with wooden blinds and a safety grid to protect it from prying eyes and snipers. Lifting a strip, she peered out into the dusk, as if she could pierce the darkness just by looking.

"They should have been back with him by now," he snarled, and she hid her sardonic smile.

"You should have sent me instead," she purred in a deep and resonate tone, dropping the blind and turning to face her erstwhile boss and sometimes lover. Lowering her chin, hair cascaded into her eyes and she gave him the smoldering look that said she alone dared to second guess his judgment. "If you wanted the job done right, that is."

Rushman waved the big stogie in his hand before knocking ashes into an empty tin. "Forget it Doll. You're too important to waste on a punk like Noble. The boys will do fine with that. He just needs a bit of convincing."

"It shouldn't be taking them this long," she said, dropping the butt on the floor and grinding it out with a boot heel, "Not with that many involved. You wouldn't have any witnesses if you caught him alone like I suggested, and used just the right kind of persuasion." A knife slid from an arm sheath, and she tested the edge before one-handedly tucking it back with a flip of the wrist and expert finger pressure.

He took a deep drag and blew out a cloud of noxious smoke before answering. "Yeah well, you have your ways, and we have ours. I need this guy alive and intact, and you're not the only one who knows how to make a man cooperate. Besides, the more people that see what happens when someone tries snubbing me, the less trouble any of them fools will give me later," he added in an ominous tone.

She shrugged noncommittally, and sauntered back to the table to give the maps one last going over. "We've got to do this before the cold weather sets in, so you'd better get his cooperation soon. If he gets away and they sail off, you'll never catch him."

"Yeah, yeah, I know." Rushman leaned forward and, setting his stogie down in an empty can, banged a button buzzer, snorting appreciatively as the house boy pounded up the stairs two at a time. "Miguel, send Tony, Rizzo, and a few of the other boys out to see what happened to those clowns we sent after Noble," he snapped at the uneasy kid with a cut lip and spiky hair who was a wannabe tough. Miguel nodded and was gone as fast as he came.

"Vixy," Rushman barked again, turning back to her, ignoring the lifted eyebrow that said she thought he'd done too little too late. "Why don't you head out and see what happened to those three foreigners that came in today on the *Solstice*. The captain seemed pretty tight with the tall doxy. If we can bring one of them in, he might be convinced to come to us himself with Noble in trade."

"On it already," she said, and glided out the door, glad to be out of

"Yeah well, you have your ways, and we have ours."

Rushman's oppressive presence, and away from the smelly office. There wasn't anything Vixen Macall, renowned treasure and bounty hunter, smuggler, as well as one of the shadowy wraiths of the back alley assassins guild, wouldn't do for enough credits. Putting up with overbearing George Rushman tried her patience though. He was the only game in town these days, and he rewarded her well, so she bided her time and pretended to be the big loud slob's paramour. That allowed her to eat regularly and stay one step ahead of what was left of the feds in Columbiana. Her only other options were to ship out or turn to piracy, and she loved the land too much to remain at sea all the time.

"Once I've got enough saved to get out of this shipwreck of a town, I'm gone," she breathed in a bitter sigh before slipping into the night via the back door of what Rushman laughingly called his headquarters. "Sooner or later, somebody is going to take out that over-ambitious idiot, and I'm not going down with him."

∿

The sudden darkness was a great diversion, and David Shepherd saw his opportunity was at hand. Letting go of the garrote that was gradually choking the life from him, he went backwards and limp on purpose, trying to feign unconsciousness. Once the one wielding the choking cord relaxed his hold enough, Shepherd quickly jammed both elbows into his gut. It only knocked the wind from his assailant, but the man doubled over and both the knife and the cord slipped from his fingers.

Shepherd sprawled forward and made a grab for the blade. The wheezing man countered with a hastily swung fist to the temple, which knocked Davey sideways and gave his opponent enough time to snatch up his knife and lunge forward.

The feisty little sailor was not one to go down easily. Even with his head spinning and spots of color dancing before his eyes, he kicked out hard and connected with his attacker's knees, sweeping the man's feet out from under him and toppling him like a tree. Shepherd squirmed sideways and grabbed for the wrist holding the knife, just managing to deflect it before it sliced into his belly. The other man refused to relent, and they wound up rolling around together in a struggling, punching, and swearing tangle as they both fought for control of the blade.

∿

She regained consciousness face down in the dark, lying flat out on the cold, rubble-strewn ground. Her head was spinning and her heart raced in an irregular rhythm, skipping beats.

At first only small things registered. The sharp gravel abrading her skin, the aching of her assaulted muscles, and the smokiness of her own hair. She became aware that Alfie Noble was groaning somewhere nearby as he attempted to sit up, and a ways off, there was a scuffle and curses as David Shepherd was fighting back, though she couldn't yet raise her head to see how that was going. She lay as if dead, with only her eyes glowing faintly with a glare of defiance. For while Aleta Kalama might be stunned and confused, she was not out of this battle yet.

Fortunately for her, the blaster had jammed and discharged completely when it was dropped, and then immediately powered off into safety mode. Since the man had fired it quickly, the particle accelerator hadn't built it back up enough for a kill, and what hit her was basically a hard stun. It knocked her down, paralyzed her motor muscles, and her fire went out. Aleta lay there half in a stupor for a moment longer, feeling sickeningly dizzy and disoriented, though she now had most of her faculties about her.

She could hear a man creeping up, trying to assess whether she was actually dead or just out cold. She remained still as a corpse, waiting for the right moment. There were others with him now, at least two lingering somewhat behind, and both had voices she hadn't heard before. She let them all draw close enough for her to take them on without assistance. They were so near now, she could hear the front-most man's heavy breathing as he bent and slipped fingers to her throat to check for a pulse, though she was disappointed when the other two went after Alfie instead of her. Someone else stomped past too, intent on taking David Shepherd out of the fight.

Muscles tensed and coiled, Aleta sprang like a cat and surged upward. Her head connected hard with a man's chin, which staggered him backward long enough for her to scramble to her feet. She spun around, already crackling ablaze, noting with satisfaction that while she didn't have her full strength yet, the man behind her was already alight and yelping. He stumbled away, flailing his arms aimlessly before dropping to roll, trying desperately to beat out the undying flames that were crisping his clothing and hair, and beginning to sear his flesh.

The others had taken a few wild shots at her, but were now rapidly retreating. Their companion's unearthly shrieking and wails had completely unnerved them as his blazing form writhed in mortal agony on the ground, the flames of the spirit fire consuming him as well as lighting up the alley. Aleta had completely recovered her control and her composure. She strode past the charred and contorting corpse without even looking down, her eyes a bright incandescent orange as she lashed out at the retreating men with whips of fire. They turned tail and ran, dragging a still groggy Alfie Noble between them. She advanced on them with deadly intent, wanting to hunt down every last one of those two-bit hoods and make sure they knew there were some things in the world that were more to be feared than whomever had sent them!

~

Dimly, between blows, David Shepherd was aware he was losing his part of the battle. Their attackers had been joined by even more men, and the knife had become a moot point, for it spun away when a second man yanked him to his feet. The one beating him mercilessly was called Rizzo, a huge burly oaf that dwarfed even Alfie Noble. Each gigantic fist that crashed into his face and head looked as if it could choke the life out of a horse. Shepherd could not see how many more had arrived, for his eyes were swollen shut and he was backed against the wall with his furious captor working over his already bruised ribs and the other man's pummeling turning his face into porridge.

He was trying to duck and cover from the worst of the beating when overhead came a sudden roaring of gale force winds. Something blew past in the semi-darkness, and then a strong air current lifted the screeching mountain of Rizzo off his feet. He flew sideways, shrieking like a schoolgirl being violated before he smashed into the nearest building with a sickeningly pulpy thud. His lifeless form slid down to lay motionless in a broken heap, like a rag doll that had been tossed aside.

The man who had been working Shepherd over all evening quailed as a ghostly figure wrapped in mist landed lightly beside him. Zephirine Merriwether, dressed in a long, dark coat and billowing dress over tall boots, scowled at him as she lifted her hands with palms outward, and used a pressing north wind to pin the man who had been beating David Shepherd a good ten feet off the ground and up against the rough and rocky wall.

"Talk to me, or I'll drop you on your head somewhere in the next block. Who sent you?" she insisted, keeping the winds holding him up there under constant pressure.

"Rushman. Georgie Rushman," he yelled, trying to be heard over the roaring noise that blew his words away. "He wants Noble for a job."

So this was the dirty work of the head of the local crime syndicate, a man that everyone seemed to fear and spoke of in dread whispers.

"Go tell your boss he'd best leave us and our friends alone," she called up with more bravado than she felt. "Because if he doesn't, we're coming for him next!" She let the man slide all the way down the wall, the roughness scraping the sweat soaked shirt off his back and abrading the skin to bloody rawness. She blew him down the alley in the opposite direction, end over end, before turning back to a grinning David Shepherd, who was spitting blood and broken teeth from between swollen lips in a bruised face.

"I've never been 'appier to see a coupl'a lasses, as you and Missy Aleta," he said thickly as she helped him stand and felt around to see if there were any broken bones. "He hurt mostly me pride," he lied and winced as she probed his ribs and midsection.

"Let's get you inside," she told Shepherd, giving him a strong arm to lean on. Judging by the light bobbing their way, Aleta was on her way back.

"They got away, but they had Noble with them," the small, dark skinned woman said in a frustrated tone.

"We got to go rescue Alfie," Shepherd insisted, and he tried to pull away.

"We'll get him back," Zephirine promised as a tired and half dressed Aleta stomped over to light the way, her eyes aglow and fingertips still afire, and her slender, shivering form smelling of smoke. "But we need a plan, and I want Jordyn in on this one."

~

"You actually pinched it?" Vixy said with surprise. She was almost a bit alarmed when Will had whistled from the shadows, and flashed the case at her.

The kid nodded. "Yeah, I did. I saw them leavin' the Darkwater, and some of Big Georgie's goons was after 'em. I figured I'd get there first, before some heads got knocked in. Didn't want them dumb bozos making good with the boss and then we never sees a dime of this."

He opened the cover for her, and she gasped. The case alone was worth quite a bit, but what was inside would bring a king's ransom. She fingered each piece, lifting the gears and the planetary spheres, hefting the golden sun to feel its weight. She had not seen anything quite that elaborate in all her life; and Vixy Macall had done her share of treasure hunting over her thirty and four cycles. All that was missing was the half sphere star chart base and stand, and then it would be operational, and worth ten times ten what it was now.

She composed herself before she spoke, her tone low and reassuring. "You did good kid," she said at last, looking around to make sure no one else could see what they had. "Now find a safe place to ditch it, and make yourself scarce for the rest of the day. I want to know more about these people, and where the rest of it is. If we can put this all together, we'll be set for life."

"I know a place down under the boardwalk by the old warehouses, where no one goes. I keeps some stuff there so's the town bullies don't get it. It'll be safe enough–"

"See that it is," she warned him as he rewrapped it in the ratty knitted cloth. "This thing is our ticket out of here Willy, so don't blow it. Stay out of trouble tonight, lie low, and meet me out in the dead zone by morning." She handed him another credit and he snitched another cig before they parted company.

Vixy watched him go until his lean, rangy form disappeared in the darkness, and then she was off to the find the ones she had come looking for, leaving her last partner's son to hide the Merriwether fortune in a small niche where he kept the family holy book and his favorite loaded gaming pieces.

She headed back on her quest, making her way through the seamier part of Yorkville in the night, unfazed by the crime around her. The knife on her arm, blaster in her belt, and an extra gun in one boot gave Vixy all the security she needed.

~

"So… you're asking me to join some kind of guardian force that you send out to save these pure humans from themselves," Roan commented wryly as he watched the dereliction and depravity unfolding around them. He turned liquid brown eyes toward the demi-god at his side, who had been watching him curiously after laying out the details of the elemental team he was assembling. "Why bother? They don't seem to care what kind of life they have."

"Not all humans are like that Roan," Jordyn said in a low, soothing voice. "Many are good people just trying to survive in a world torn apart by wars and climate change that they had nothing to do with. Their governments have collapsed. Their gods have abandoned them, and they need someone to look up to again. Someone strong and fair minded, with their best interests at heart."

"Humans just like these people let my mother die alone, just because my father was a selkie," Roan reminded Jordyn in a bitter tone. "And she was one of them! They wouldn't let her live with them because she had consorted with what they considered a demon. Mother was a very faithful woman. She taught me all about the great sky god, and his supposed love for all, even me. Yet when she sent me off to beg the parish priest to confess her before she died, he wouldn't come down to the shore and she was too weak and sick to walk all the way into town. So she died a sinner, and unloved by her own people."

His jaw tightened, remembering that sad night long ago. "People like them," he waved a furred arm to indicate the entire town of Yorkville, "They don't want my help. They like how they live. They hunt my friends of the sea for food, or make them do dangerous things like finding ship mines." He thought of Free, who had left him to join the wild ones of her own kind, wondering how she fared these days. "I see no reason why I should work hard to save them from themselves."

Jordyn bowed his head. The Finnman had obviously had a hard life. The last of the Orions knew he would have to be far more persuasive. Sometimes it was hard to put into words those things he felt so deeply that he knew it with his soul rather than with any sort of rational thought.

"I can't say that I blame you Roan, not after all you've lived through so far. Still, you have to understand that sometimes when the need is dire, we must do what is best for the majority without being selective. If we are ever to have peace on Earth, we must be brave and fight for it. I believe we who have extraordinary powers or talents are blessed with them because we are so desperately needed, and accordingly we must make the best use of those blessings without thinking of who will benefit most, or even if anyone will truly appreciate what we do. We need to set an example that brings hope back into the human heart. We should show them that if we work together, we can take back this world."

"Now you sound like mother. She always thought the best of people, no matter how ill they treated her," Roan said with a sigh and a faraway look, remembering how fervently she had prayed for her people, the very ones who had turned her out. "She never gave up hope that she could turn their hearts and minds, even when they called her names and threw garbage and old fish heads at her. I don't even know why she cared. They did not deserve her." The set of his jaw was hard, but a hand with lightly webbed fingers came up and brushed away a stray tear. It did not go unnoticed.

Jordyn's voice was soothing and low. "It sounds to me as if you loved your mother, and that she was a wise woman who taught you well. But tell me, did she speak to you of the Apocalypse?" he asked pointedly as they walked away from a plaintive street beggar who was trying to angle for a few credits to pay off his 'dear sister's debts'. Jordyn had flipped him a tiny coil of salvaged silver wire and the man ran off to the nearest gin mill to buy himself a dram of comfort.

Roan nodded slowly. "She said that the End Times would come when the world was filled with wicked people and evil deeds. After the plagues and wars, Judgment would be called. Then the Horsemen would appear to those left behind. The dead will rise, the believers will be called to heaven, and the remainder will be scourged. Mother said before she died that the End Times were upon us, but I've seen no Horsemen yet," he added with a shrug.

"They won't gather together until the final battle, but the Apocalypsians are here," Jordyn stated with conviction as they walked the rough pavement side by side, stepping over sprawled bodies lying in vomit and dodging urine puddles. "And they do far more than cull and judge humans these days. They will ruin what is left of this world—enslaving all who survive—if someone doesn't stop them. This place is just one example of that. The Elohim is gone with those who were chosen. The Elder Gods are back vying for souls, and the Apocalypsians have slipped in amongst them. I've seen Samael with my own eyes; I've spoken to him and I know his mind. But we fought him and the Children of Ba'al, and we won," he added proudly.

"The Death Lord? And you lived to talk about it?" Roan asked skeptically. "I find that hard to believe…"

"Watch this," Jordyn said, pulling the Eye of Providence from his shirt. Concentrating a bit, he slowed the swirling haze within until it cleared. When Roan looked within, it showed snippets of Jordyn's and Aleta's encounters with the undead and the showdown with Samael, as well as their battles on *Solstice* with the Atlantean Mermen and the pirates. "We took heavy losses and it was a struggle each time, but we triumphed in each instance, and the world became a little bit better place because of it," he added to Roan's wondering look.

"Then you really are heroes," Roan said quietly, and with reverence.

"And you could be one too, my boy," Jordyn suggested, with a smile and a pat on the back. "We all need something to live for. Come with us, and we shall do great things, and you won't be forgotten like your mother was. I promise you that," he added, trying to catch Roan's eyes with his own piercing aquamarine gaze.

"I'll think about it," Roan said as they continued to walk on. The idea of doing something important with his life was intriguing, but he was a timid soul, not particularly given to things involving bloodshed and heroics.

"Please do," Jordyn said in a distracted voice as he thought he heard someone step into the roadway somewhere behind them. "We're going to need all the help we can get!"

Confrontations and Complications

A few discrete questions and Vixy was advised that the blond fool who had debarked the Solstice earlier that day had recently minced by, leading some furry mutant Down Sodom. That might be where the others were headed, and so she decided to follow them.

She thought of the prize her little partner had secured for them, and smiled. Willy was a good kid, he always came through. If everything else went as well as it already had, they'd be out of there and into a new life within a fortnight.

~

The usual bias against mutants was as applicable Down Sodom as it would be anywhere else on Earth. No one would let Roan into their establishment to eat, so Jordyn had bought him some greasy fried food in a paper cone, and watched the Finnman picking away at it listlessly as they walked the silent back streets. Once they got to the far end of the red lantern district they began to angle back toward the more pedestrian part of town where Aleta and Zephirine had rooms. In spite of the deserted after midnight streets, it became apparent that they had attracted the wrong kind of attention.

"Someone is behind us, walking quietly," Roan warned Jordyn in a low, worried voice. His acute hearing had picked up the sound of stealthy footfalls almost immediately once they left the noisier area behind.

"Well, I'm not at all surprised," Jordyn answered in a low voice, for he was well aware that they had been tailed as soon as they exited Down Sodom. He had figured Roan's appearance would draw some negative attention, and that was half his reason for parading him through the area. "I just wonder what took them so long!"

"You were expecting to be followed?" Roan asked curiously, as he half turned to look behind them.

Jordyn put a warning hand on his arm. "Well, of course!" he answered in a low, bemused tone. "My team and I are heroes after all, and that gives us a lot of positive attention. The local strong arms don't like to be upstaged. And of course you are not the most popular person here..." He said it kindly, but Roan bowed his head in shame anyway. "Oh I wouldn't be too conscience-stricken about that my boy, it's just a simple fact of life. Average humans tend to fear the anomalies of their world. Whatever you do though, don't give away that we're on to the fact that we're being pursued—at least not yet. Face forward, walk confidently, but remain alert." They picked up the pace, but not enough to seem like they were in a hurry.

"Who are they?" Roan asked with a bit of alarm in his tone, though he did manage to keep his voice low.

"The word 'they' implies plural," Jordyn corrected, "Actually, there's just the one, and he–" He reached into his shirt and slipped the Eye of Providence into one hand, cupping it in front of him. It glowed softly and he peered into it with great interest, discerning things only he could understand. "I mean *she* is not all that heavily armed. Perhaps you have an admirer after all," he added, trying to break the tension.

"I doubt that," Roan said with sarcasm. "I'm only half-selkie, and as you can see, I've never been welcomed ashore."

"Then she must be after me, so I will handle this," Jordyn said with very little concern, and he spun around, holding the Eye on high. Its light shone out in the darkness, illuminating every little corner and crevice. "Come out, come out, wherever you are!" he called in a sing-song voice with one hand on his hip, and his head cocked sideways. "We already know you're there anyway."

Vixy Macall stepped from behind the corner of a building, her blaster leveled. "I have a message for you from my boss. He says to bring Noble in, and you can all leave this town in one piece. If you don't cooperate, no one's going anywhere."

"How very medieval of him," Jordyn said with a raised eyebrow. "I haven't the foggiest idea of whom or what you are speaking, but that said; I don't believe he has the right to demand anyone's surrender, at least not from us. But I'll pass it along just in case."

She never said another word, just shot the Eye from his grasp, and it spun off into the gutter. Jordyn looked surprised, and then he disappeared in a blinding flash.

Vixy strode over and with gloved hands, picked up the glowing, winking gem, and tossed it into a bag that hung from her hip. She turned and leveled the blaster at the furry freak that had been walking with the capricious little androgyne.

"Tell them to bring Noble in," she said, waving the blaster in his direction.

Roan stood with his mouth open and eyes wide for a half a moment, and then tore off through the town, running headlong for the sea and the only safety he had ever known.

~

Once they were back in their rooms, and Davey Shepherd's visible wounds had been treated with hot water and tea leaves made into poultices, Zephirine decided his ribs were likely cracked and his chest needed binding. "I have plenty of old clothes in my trunk I can rip up, I'll dig something out," she said.

"We should get after Alfie, 'fore they off him," Shepherd said thickly through cracked lips and broken teeth as he struggled to rise.

"We will," Aleta said in a soothing voice as she pushed him gently back down so she could finish dressing one of the larger cuts on his chin, after moistening again the poultice over his swollen shut eye. "They wanted him for something, so he will stay alive longer than you will if we don't tend to those wounds." She had washed out all the grit and dirt embedded in his cuts and gashes, and with a tiny little flame on one finger, cauterized them closed now that they were hopefully clean. Even the water in that town was not to be trusted, though she had boiled it good and hot. He jerked and swore under his breath as the little flames seared his raw flesh, but otherwise took it like a man.

Zephirine stood stock still. "That doesn't look the way I left it!" she said with her heart pounding in her chest.

"What doesn't look right?" Aleta said with concern, and turned to see what the other woman was talking about.

"My trunk!" Zephirine snapped. Crossing the floor with a candle holder in hand, something struck her as wrong with it. The lid was closed but the hasp was popped up and cloth was sticking out of one end. Zephirine was too fastidious for that, and she knew she had been the last one in and out of the room.

"Dammit!" she swore, "Someone's been in here!" She fell to her knees before it, and raising the lid, began to frantically pore through the contents, swearing like a dockworker. "Why didn't I notice this before? Crap for the birds, I've been robbed!" she said with a catch in her throat as she tossed things out of the trunk.

"Are you sure?" Aleta asked with alarm. Setting down the steaming kettle of water on their little methane stove, she hurried over to help Zephirine look through things. "You might have just forgotten to shut it properly. We were kind of in a hurry," she added, inclining her head toward David Shepherd, who sat up attentively with one eye still covered by the poultice and his face all puffy and bruised.

"Yes I'm sure because I didn't even look in here, and I don't leave things messy like this. Plus my orrery is definitely gone," the taller woman said with disgust as she stood up slowly. "So unless Jordyn came in while were fighting crime out back," she waved an arm toward the wall of the room that faced the alley, "and walked off with it without telling me, I'll bet that little gutter rat he had haul the trunk up here lifted it." She turned back toward the others with an anguished look. "That skinny kid is the only other one that would have known about it, and he knew right where to look too."

"I suppose it was very valuable?" Aleta queried with a sigh. The poultice hit the floor with a splat as Shepherd started to rise; his battered face now set in a scowl. He groaned a bit as he tried to lever himself off a settee that was no more than a confiscated church pew with a couple of lumpy cushions.

"Priceless," Zephirine said in a reverent whisper, as she turned to face them. Her face was ashen and she was shaking as she leaned against the trunk with her arms crossed on her chest. "It's been in my family since the Nineteenth Century. Some great-great granduncle on the Merriwether side was supposed to have been gifted of it by a wise benefactor, and he took it on his mapmaking journeys across Columbiana. When he died of mysterious circumstances, it passed to my side of the family. They all claimed the base was missing when it was shipped back to us, and that part was never seen again. Before the Global Wars, my grandpap saw a picture of the base in a museum catalog from this area, but he never was able to raise the cash to come overseas and claim it, and they didn't answer his inquiries via the post. You know how things went in those days," she added sadly, and slumped forward disconsolately. "Grandpap died not long after, but he had already given what was left of the orrery to Daddy, and Daddy gave it to me. I came here to see if I could find the base and make it operational again, but I didn't think everything would be as ruined over here as it is. And now it's gone too…"

David Shepherd was already heading for the door. "Don't you fret Miss Zee," his voice thick from a swollen jaw. "I'll go after 'im Love, and we'll get yer whatever ya call it back." He was walking stiffly and with a limp. "We also got to rescue me mate Alfie," he added, holding his arm to his chest and wincing in pain.

"Not before we bind those ribs of yours," Aleta insisted, and she and Zephirine got busy ripping up an old petticoat to make impromptu windings, which he grudgingly submitted to.

"And I want a change of clothing," Zephirine said, yanking a tight pair of leggings from the trunk's contents. "No more fighting in dresses!"

"You have a point there," Aleta said, finishing Shepherd's bandage and scavenging something for herself. "Too much wall climbing in this business!"

That was a hard thought. Had cleaning out demons and crime elements, and rescuing good people caught in bad circumstances, really become their life and livelihood?

"Why does everything have to be so damnably hard?" Zephirine complained as they locked the door behind them and headed back out into the night.

"Just the way the world is these days," Aleta answered, and David Shepherd grunted affirmatively as he stumped heavily down the stairwell behind them.

"Surely makes ye appreciate the good times, don' it?" he added, but the girls were already well ahead of him, planning their strategy.

~

"What you got for me Doll?" Georgie Rushman said curiously as Vixy took the gently glowing orb out of a small sack with a gloved hand and a rag and placed it carefully on the nightstand. As much as he hated the way she could just slip in and out of his place at will, he was intrigued that she'd brought him a gift.

"A little present I picked up Down Sodom," she said with a smile. It was nothing she had intended to part with, but she had to give him something else to focus on besides the fact that she hadn't succeeded in bringing in any of the trio of strangers from *Solstice*.

He eyed it suspiciously. He'd never seen anything like it before. Even though it was round, it didn't roll, and the soft light it gave off illuminated the entire predawn bedroom. "What's it for?"

"I'm not sure," she answered honestly, and while his attention was on it, palmed something else that was in her pocket. "It seems to be some kind of self-contained lightning source—but don't touch it!" she warned, leaning down to push him away with one slender hand while the other slid an item just under the covers. "I had leather gloves on and it was burning my skin right through them, and it's not even on high power. I've seen it far brighter." She showed him her original gloves, the palms all twisted and shrunken. "But it didn't burn anything that wasn't touching skin. It's also very heavy for its size. I figured you'd want to see this right away, so I dropped what I was doing to bring it in." It was a lie, but a plausible one.

"Great, so what do I do with it?" he said, sitting up to watch her kick off her boots. That meant she was coming to bed with him, a rare but welcome pleasure. He had to wipe the drool from his chin folds as he contemplated the possibilities.

She sighed and wondered how he ever got to be as high in the organization as he was. "Have your eggheads study it and see if they can figure out how it works. This thing would probably shine that way even underwater, so it could prove useful."

The dawning realization on his face showed he understood. "Divers would be able to use them as lanterns during recovery missions."

"Exactly," she said, glad he had finally gotten the idea.

"How'd you get it?" he asked pointedly, with that feral sly look that said he wanted a straight answer, though one big hand was already fondling her oh-so firm buttocks.

She measured her answer carefully, and let him do a little more booty grabbing than she would normally tolerate to keep him from thinking too hard. "One of the freaks down there dropped it, and I figured it was worth more than chasing after those friends of Noble's would be."

He nodded. "It is. We've got most of what we need now, with this little gadget."

She sat on the bed and leaned against him, letting him slip a meaty hand into her blouse, trying not to wince at his cold, pinching fingers. "So, did they did bring him in after all?" she inquired. Having Noble under wraps would solve a lot of problems, especially if some of his friends wound up in the harbor. That way no one would be left who might mention that precious little artifact Willy had pilfered earlier. Just to make sure Rushman's attention was more on some prurient possibilities than what she was saying, she reached over and gave his pulpy groin a playful squeeze before she began undoing snaps and fasteners slowly and seductively, revealing a few inches of creamy flesh at a time.

Rushman moved over, to watch with greedy little porcine eyes, and then patted a spot next to him. She shrugged out of her clothing and tossed it aside, surreptitiously sliding something under the pillow in the process.

"Yeah, the boys finally got him, but not without a helluva fight. Some wild story they told though. Supposedly tangled with a woman that could shoot out fires, and some kind of witch that can fly. I'd say those guys were drunk or strung out, except I seen Coltrane's back all scraped raw from where he said the flying witch pushed him up the wall with wind from her fingers, and Tony's hands were blistered from trying to help put out the fire that killed Jo Jo. *He* burnt to a crisp, and Rizzo's dead as a doornail from hitting a building pretty hard, so I dunno what the devil happened out there." He actually looked worried.

"So where's Noble now?" Vixy purred as she dropped the last of her underthings before slowly crawling in next to his big hairy, bloated body in the bed. While he was ogling her, a slender hand lightly ran over his chest and belly and then slyly slipped lower, and she noted the shiver of anticipation and rigidity as he tossed the sheets back. She quickly moved up to straddle and mount him, because taking the command position would dictate what would happen next.

His voice sounded strained as she began to rock slowly but sensuously back and forth. "He's in the w-wine cellar... tied d-down to a chair and c-chilling out... They–they're going back to f-find his friends, b–because I don't... I d-don't want... *Oh baby you're good!* I don't want no-no witnesses, y-you know? *Not so fast, slow down damn you or I'll lose it right away!*"

"So get in the driver's seat if you don't like it my way," she said coyly, knowing he preferred to be in charge all the time and was no longer willing to wait.

Rushman roughly flipped her onto her back, and she slid something out from under the pillow into one hand, flipping the cap off while moaning extravagantly and arching upwards. His voice drifted off into animal grunts and heavy breathing along with the rhythmic slapping of flesh and creaking of the big wooden bed. She moved her arms around his back and up his neck, hands pressing into the rolls of fat, urging him on. He was covered in sweat and almost sliding off her when the shuddering and

She shrugged out of her clothing

thrusting ended in a victorious howl of triumph, and he slumped sideways.

He never even noticed the prick of the needle in the side of his neck. She palmed it and let it drop off the bed, onto the wolf skin rug he'd had imported at great expense from the wild northern lands.

"*You are something–*" Big Georgie Rushman started to say as he flopped over onto his back, but then he jerked and choked, gasping for air a couple of times. His eyes went wide, rolling back into his head while he clawed at his chest. His body spasmed and stiffened as his inability to breathe abruptly stopped his heart.

When she was sure he was completely paralyzed, Vixy pulled herself free, and stood up to put on her clothing. When she was dressed again, she looked down on George Rushman's blank, blue-toned face one last time with a sardonic smile.

"Yeah, I am something, aren't I?" she said in a low voice filled with bitterness. "But I'm still alive and now you're dead as that city out there. That's for having Walter Teller killed just so you could get me all to yourself. I'm just returning the favor." She laughed mirthlessly as she yanked the covers over his stiffening body and then bent to pick up the syringe, carefully setting it on the nightstand near the orb, before hurriedly packing up. Quickly disassembled, the needle, plunger and cap went back into the false heel panels of her boots. Patting secret pockets, she made sure she had all she needed. She quickly raided her former boss' room for any spare credits he might have stowed away.

No one had seen her come in to Rushman's chambers; no one would see her leave either. She'd be back in her room and asleep well before the early morning alarm at the boss' death was raised, and she was a good enough actress to pull off feigned grief at his massive heart attack.

She grabbed up the glowing orb with one glove used as a hot pad in the palm of the other, and opened the panel in the hidden wall within the walk-in closet that lead to the eaves of the building, latching it behind her. Creeping through the darkness, the slight glow of the pulsating sphere was just enough to light her way until she reached her own room again.

~

Knowing the town fairly well, Shepherd made a few discrete inquiries. No one claimed to have seen Alfie Noble, but almost everyone knew where the boy who hired out as a hauler lived. They also knew the woman he called 'Aunt Vixy' worked for Big Georgie and that nobody trusted her.

The three of them were directed back to a flophouse above a raucous sa-loon Down Sodom where the kid slept. He wasn't home and it was well after midnight, and David was worse for wear, so Aleta and Zephirine insisted he hunker down to wait for the boy while they went out on the streets to hunt for him.

"I don' like leavin' ye both on yer own, there's a lot of bad out there," he said glumly.

Zephirine shook her head and sighed. "You need the rest David. Besides, you'd best worry more about what *we'll* do to anyone who troubles us any further this night."

David Shepherd couldn't argue with that; not after what he'd seen these two special ladies do to anything or anyone who had attacked them.

"Go then. I'll stay and wait, but I'm not promising I won't wring his bloody neck if he shows up."

"Fine, just don't do it before you find out where my orrery is," Zephirine answered in a parting shot, and she blew him a kiss before she shut the warped door to the ramshackle flat behind her.

For a town as strung out as Yorkville was, it didn't take long to find the boy. Willy Teller was always ready to make a fast buck and was as bad at gambling as his father had been. He'd been out the rest of the night, and lost all that Vixy had given him playing with the hexagonal dice; even with his loaded pair he lost most of his tosses. He came sauntering back home in the wee hours before dawn, whistling softly down the dark street, ready to run if one of the demons or derelicts that haunted the area ap-proached him for a handout, or worse. He'd seen the harbor freak that night walking around with that cocky little clown with glowing aquama-rine eyes that had paid him a few paltry ship pieces to haul the tall lady's trunk. They had kind of spooked him, showing up together like that, and he was nervous about having those searching eyes turned his way.

So when the small, thin, dark skinned woman in tight slacks stepped out in front of Willy, he stopped cold and stared at her. She might be one of the local strumpets, but she looked familiar, though the fire in her eyes and the little flames dancing in her left hand said she was definitely some-thing else.

"Where's my orrery boy?" asked another woman's reproachful voice from behind him. A cold wind whipped forth and blew his hair around, making him shiver.

"I dunno what you're talkin' about!" Willy said as he edged away. As the fire-bearing woman came forward he leapt the gutter to run, and landed right in David Shepherd's arms.

"Oh yes ye do—yer stinkin', thievin' hands are all over this one, ye little filcher! Ye better tell us what that happened to me mate Alfie Noble too, or I swear I be taking it out o' yer miserable hide." The man's thick voice was pitched low and harsh as he cuffed the shaking kid soundly.

"David, you were supposed to stay put tonight," Aleta said reproachfully. "We've got this."

"I know ye do Aleta Darlin', but this kind of local scum don' answer questions unless ye give him a little incentive," Shepherd said as he twisted an arm behind the youngster's back and whirled him around. He shoved a scuffling and struggling Willy ahead of him toward where the two women awaited, a battered hand with scabbed over knuckles gripping the boy's thin shoulder while the other hand held the opposite arm at a very uncomfortable angle. "Keep moving laddie, or I'll break yer arm like kindlin'," he warned.

"Don't beat me, it ain't my fault! I had to steal it 'cause Aunt Vixy owed Big Georgie, and he'd a had her kilt! We gotta eat and stuff you know," Willy added, trying to look as pitiful as possible at the two frowning women while bracing to kick the man behind him in the groin with a boot heel and make a run for it. "And I don't know nothin' about what happened to that big ox you were with, 'cause I was too busy runnin' away to care."

He attempted the back kick, but David Shepherd was on to him and dodged while dragging him around to face his own furious expression. "Stealing ain't your only sin you scrawny liar," he said, as a quick clip to the chin toppled Willy and he landed face up on the ground.

Zephirine came up and immediately yanked the young man to his feet by one arm. She brought her furious face close to his own, the wind coming off her whistling in his ears. Her hazel eyes were cold and hard as flint.

"I don't believe you gave anything away that you could fence for yourself elsewhere. Now you're going to take us to where you hid my orrery, and then you're taking us to this Big Georgie's place. If you behave yourself, we'll let you go. If you give me any trouble," she spun him around until he could see Aleta, who limned her body with fire for a moment, "I'll let her handle it from there on in."

His eyes went wide at Aleta all aflame before Willy Teller hung his head. He shuffled his feet, saying nothing initially, but nodding slowly. Oh, Vixy was going to kill him for this!

"We gotta head down by the docks, I hid your case there. Big Georgie's place is a far bit from that, on the other side of Down Sodom behind where the old warehouses are," he said with a resolute sigh as David Shepherd grabbed his arm again and propelled him forward.

"I'm tired of this town already," Aleta grumbled, stifling a big yawn as she and Zephirine brought up the rear. "We haven't had a moment's peace!"

"And where in Hades is Jordyn?" Zephirine added. "He's certainly making himself scarce!"

The boy purposely never mentioned having seen the mysterious Master Orion when he was Down Sodom with the furry sea freak. Vixy always said, when questioned, never volunteer anything you aren't asked directly.

As they passed by, a few faces peeked out of windows in concern. One pair of eyes also watched from the water before a silent, sleek form dove down and followed them along the shoreline, hoping that these people would find out for him what happened to the now missing Numen they had come ashore with.

~

On Georgie Rushman's nightstand within the Eye of Providence, Jordyn Orion had gotten a voyeur's view to all that had transpired. He was aware that this was more than a tryst that ended badly. It was a successful coup attempt, and he surmised that this clever female was about to take over her leader's crime operation. He decided to wait it out a bit and see what she had in mind before making his presence known. If nothing else, it might give him some idea what kind of hierarchy the local syndicate had, and in truth he found this capable woman rather intriguing. So as she traveled through the walls to the room of her own on the opposite side of the building he let the Eye remain as an innocuous and very warm, glowing sphere.

He gave no indication of his presence once they reached her rather austere but comfortable apartment. She barred the eave doorway, and piled clothing and gear in front of it. He did not protest when she locked him in a drawer along with her weaponry and other tools of the trade. Jordyn waited patiently for her to undress and fall asleep, and then stayed within the Eye, immobile inside the drawer, expecting some alarms to sound so he could slip off unnoticed.

"I wish they'd get on with this charade," he grumbled as the hours dragged by. It seemed no one regularly checked on the big boss, though he was supposed to have guards all over the building. Jordyn risked sending out a wisp of sensory tentacle from the Eye and it passed through the drawer's lock and out into the room. A small head, like that of a serpent, formed on the end of the ectoplasm, forming eyes, nose, ears, and antennae to take readings of the surroundings, sending the information back to the rest of his essence within the orb.

It was predawn, judging by the light that leaked around the sides of the shades covering the windows. The woman slept lightly in the nearby bed, sprawled out with her hair spilling over the pillow, but her right hand was beneath where she kept a hidden blaster. A belt with a knife in the scabbard hung on the bedpost. Her clothes were casually draped over the back of a chair, and a dressing gown was tossed on the edge of the bed, slippers beneath. The rest of the room was neat and orderly, as if she hadn't a care in the world. The door to the hallway was securely locked, and only faint light seeped underneath, indicating a window out there somewhere.

Jordyn was just withdrawing his feeler when there was the sound of heavy footfalls and a vigorous pounding that woke the woman up immediately. "I'm coming," she called sleepily and rolled out of bed. He zipped the tendril back inside as Vixy Macall, blaster in hand, snatched up her gown and shrugged it over her nightwear before padding to the door. She checked the peephole before undoing the lock and deadbolt, though she kept it chained.

"What's up Marley; you look like you saw a ghost," she commented, shoving the hair out of her eyes.

"A demon!" the old man who acted as a butler said with his eyes big and round. "It came into the yard all afire, and it took out Sol and Tully before they could get a bead on it. Now it's headed this way," he added with dread, and crossed himself. Marley was an Xtian, steeped in the old faith.

"I'll be right down. Go wake the boss, and get him out of here!" she snapped, and shut the door in his face. Things were going to get complicated if they had some kind of renegade mutant inside the walled yard. Her first thought was to secure her claim on the business, before someone found Rushman dead and tried to usurp her. She opened the drawer where the Eye was and, grabbing a piece of clothing to handle it with, hurriedly poked it and several other items into a backpack. Dressing quickly, she was ready to go in minutes, heading straight for the cellar where Alfie Noble should still be tied. He was her ticket to the treasure of a lifetime, and no way was Vixen Macall losing out on that!

Showdown!

With David Shepherd shoving him along, Willy Teller lead them right toward his stash. His idea was to crawl underneath the boardwalk and disappear into the nearby rocks and rubble with the precious artifact he had pilfered for Vixy. He surmised from the stiff way the man was moving, the bruises on his face, and the snippets of conversation he had picked up, that *Solstice's* new captain had already run afoul of Big Georgie's thugs. So Shepherd should be no challenge to elude; and as long as Willy got a good head start against the two witches, they would never catch him.

"I have to get below, and crawl along a bit. It's kinda tight," he explained, his face all innocence.

"I'll go with him," Aleta said, and she dropped down the side of the boardwalk with the boy and crawled underneath. "Lots of big spiders down here," she said with distaste, burning off web after web as she crouched along behind Willy, who took advantage of her squeamishness to edge away from her.

"Don't be lettin' that guttersnipe get ahead of ye," Shepherd warned as he followed Aleta's glow through the cracks above. "He'll likely bolt as soon as ye take eyes off 'im." He didn't trust the boy at all, and neither did Zephirine, who paced restlessly at his side, her long legged stride in boots and leggings slowed down to match David's bowlegged gimp.

"We're almost there," Willy announced as he went down on all fours. He had dragged in a small waterproof composite crate from one of the warehouses to hold his valuables, and hid it half buried in the sand of a protected spot, covered with old seaweed. He carefully removed the shawl covered brass case, and put the covering back before turning to see where the fire woman was.

"Ack! One of the blasted things dropped into my hair!" Aleta yelped and she lit up involuntarily, burning the spider out and scorching the boards overhead before she could regain control. Shepherd and Zephirine had to jump back as little flames licked up through the slats of that section of boardwalk.

That was when Willy made his break for it. He emerged from the other side of the broad wooden walkway with the case under his arm and scrambled out onto the small spit of rocky beach. Vaulting rocks, rubble, and driftwood, he headed down the shoreline as fast as his flying feet could take him.

"He's getting away!" Aleta shouted as she pushed her way back around the pilings and tried to exit after the boy, her flames burning brightly. She couldn't keep up with his pounding pace, and constantly tripped over things that the glow around her obscured.

"'E's headin' down ashore—around the inlet!" David Shepherd yelled back and tried to find a spot where he could leap safely off the walkway and not break any more bones.

Zephirine shouldered him aside.

"I'll bring that devious little brat back in," she said with conviction as she stepped forward. The predawn blush in the distance gave her just enough light to work by. Feet spread and arms extended, palms at an angle, she summoned the winds to wrap filaments around the fleet footed boy.

Willy slowed and then stopped, legs paddling but unable to make any headway against the encircling crosscurrents that were buffeting him backwards. Just as he reached the opposite side of the inlet, Zephirine began to reel him in. He fought and struggled mightily, and almost escaped more than once, because Zephirine was exhausted after a long day and night without more than a catnap before dinner. But she was also very angry and quite determined not to let her orrery fall into the wrong hands. Eventually the net of winds lifted the lightweight lad off his feet and dragged him over the water and landscape back toward the boardwalk where his captor waited with a very deep scowl on her face.

She dumped him unceremoniously on the rough wood at David Shepherd's feet. The equally angry man lifted a struggling and wild eyed young man by his collar, and cuffed him soundly before setting him down roughly. He was notably empty handed.

"What did you do with my property boy?" Zephirine said with a snarl, as she got right in his face.

"I dropped it when the winds lifted me," he said through chattering teeth, all the fight having gone out of him. He was quaking in terror. "It fell in the water when I was flying back here–" He winced and ducked as David's hand clamped down on his shoulder again.

"I'd like te wring yer scrawny little neck! Ye deserve no better than that fer all the 'ardship ye caused tonight." The boy was silent, but he shrank away, not so much from the threat of the man behind him, but the tall, frowning witch with the wild brown hair and long coat lifting in the breeze that always seemed to play around her.

"Tie him up or something," Zephirine said brusquely and strode away, for she saw her fiery companion had made it to the water's edge and stood peering out to sea. She ran lightly down the boardwalk, leaping over the burned area, and headed toward where a now extinguished Aleta was talking with someone half in and out of the water. And as she drew closer she could tell that the swimmer was holding the case to her orrery!

"This is yours?" the lightly furred man with faint freckling asked as he handed the wet and dripping brass case to Zephirine, who had clambered down to join Aleta on the rocky sand.

"Yes, it is! And thank you for retrieving it," she said with relief, opening it up to reveal the contents a bit damp but otherwise intact. "I can't tell you what it means to me to get this back…" Her voice trailed off and her eyes were damp and misty.

"It's very old, and of another world," her benefactor said slowly, hanging his head in embarrassment over how her words made him ache to hold her close. "If the Harbormaster knew of it, he would rise and take it from you," he added with seriousness and a worried frown that crinkled his lightly plush brow. "He has the missing part in his cave," he added. "I've seen it and it has power about it! The fish people wanted it, but he refused to give it up, and they threatened him. Now he doesn't let them come too close."

The women looked at each other and Zephirine shrugged. They had no idea what he was talking about, but suspected he meant something involving the local crime boss having secured the base of the orrery for himself. The term 'fish people' sounded like the Atlantean mermen. Since they were on their way to see the man they suspected was the Harbormaster anyway, they let that reference to the Atlanteans go. As far as Zephirine's orrery being of another world; that could simply mean it predated the global conflicts. Mutants tended to see things differently than humans, since they seldom shared the same history.

"What's this bloomin' freak doin' ashore?" David Shepherd asked when he caught up with them. He had cut someone's boat mooring line and trussed Willy Teller's hands behind his back and hobbled his ankles so that the boy could walk, but not escape again. "They'll run 'im off if they see 'im!

"I only came in tonight because the Orion Numen asked me to," Roan said petulantly.

"You've seen Jordyn?" Zephirine and Aleta said together, and Roan nodded.

"He took me into the back part of town, bought me food, and told me all about you. How you fight and the good things you do. He wanted me to join with you–" He had begun to walk out of the water, but stopped when he saw Shepherd's frowning face, and the two women's looks of alarm. His rather prominent state of arousal had just become noticeable.

"Git ye gone, ye filthy, furry beast," Shepherd said with a threatening growl.

Roan began to retreat, his wary brown eyes keeping a close watch on David Shepherd, who didn't appear to be armed, but still sounded dangerous.

Aleta turned and glared at Davey, her eyes glowing lightly with anger. "This is an acquaintance of Jordyn's who rescued Zephirine's astro-thing from the water."

"Ah, don' ye believe a word 'e says. This one is well known around the nor'east coast as a thief and a beggar, as well as a threat to women. Folks 'round here don' take kindly to none of that," Shepherd added, giving a Willy a hard shake as a reminder that he too had better be listening.

"Well I don't care, because he's been a friend to me today. Do you have a name?" Zephirine called after the rapidly retreating form, who was sinking into the rising tide lapping at their feet.

"Roan... Roan Finnman," he said before upending and disappearing from sight. The boats would be out soon and he didn't want to be reported to the seal gunners.

"Thank you Roan!" Zephirine called out after him, and when his head bobbed up some yards distant, both she and Aleta waved, before turning to head resolutely inland toward where a much abashed Willy Teller said Big Georgie Rushman's place was located.

"He's got a lot o' goons that are good shots," the young man warned them.

"These ladies be not much worried about that," Shepherd said with wry reverence. "Them ruffians t'wont be a match for 'em, if we get the drop on 'em!"

Just to be on the safe side, as they drew near to the crime boss' residence, David tore a sleeve from his already dirty and ragged shirt, and gagged Willy so he could not cry out a warning.

"What do we do with this?" Aleta said to Zephirine once they had left Willy and David behind. She pointed down, indicating the case containing the orrery.

"Let me show you something else that no one but my family knows about," Zephirine whispered softly. She strode over to where an old rowboat that had rotted had been pulled well up the beach, and set the case down on it. Looking around, she could see no one nearby, and David Shepherd was out of earshot, with his back to them while he further trussed up a muffled squawking Willy well out on an old abandoned dock, where he wouldn't be seen or heard for quite some time. "This thing can be hidden for quite a while this way if you remember how to properly key it up," she added, realizing that was one thing she hadn't taken the time to do before they went out to dinner. Depressing the jeweled eyes while spinning the emblem like a dial, she went first one way, and then the other, counting turns. The case faded and then became part of the bleached driftwood color of the old boat.

"That's amazing!" Aleta said with awe.

"Yes it is, and it will stay that way until someone who knows the code and where to look for it comes to retrieve it," Zephirine said with satisfaction as she tucked it underneath. "I guess I forgot to do that before we went out for the evening."

"It's been a long voyage," Aleta said with a tired sigh as they headed back toward David Shepherd.

"It's not getting any easier now that we're ashore," Zephirine grumbled.

~

Once out of the harbor area, Roan watched the first boats leaving for the day. He really needed to eat again, but for some reason didn't follow them out to sea that day. The Numen and his lady friends with their fantastic powers intrigued him, and he was tired of living a subsistence existence.

The astronomical instrument the tall woman with the pale skin and windblown hair had thanked him for returning was very old and precious, and it had been sung about in mermaid tales. In the wrong hands, it could do some serious damage. Roan had lifted it cautiously from the water before the news of its discovery could travel far enough to be sensed by one who would kill everyone in the area to prevent it from being reassembled, for so near the sea, it would call to the fish people and they would swarm the shore town to get it, slaughtering all in their path. Jordyn Orion must know about it, and since he had fought one of the Apocalypsians already, he would be the right person to keep it. Still, it was useless without the other part, and that called to the fish people too.

"Maybe if I tell him about my new friends, The Harbormaster will trade me the missing part for one of the other treasures below," Roan said, and let the chop of the outgoing tide buffet him toward his little rocky home.

"But what would I have to give him that could be traded for it?"

There was nothing he could think of, and getting to it would be difficult with all the sharks around anyway. So he climbed out onto the rocks and sat down disconsolately, head in hands, trying to decide what to do.

~

"Are we ready for this?" Aleta asked in a whisper as she eyed the steep wall ahead of her.

"As ready as we'll ever be," Zephirine said with a resigned sigh. "But how are we going to get over there without being seen?"

David Shepherd had rejoined them after tying young Willy Teller securely to a dock post and he spoke up.

"Best way in is o'er the top. Do ye think ye can lift me with yer winds?" he asked Zephirine. She looked at him skeptically before replying.

"It's awful risky David! I didn't even know I could do it until I tried; but then, I can sense the wind beneath me. I don't know that I'd be able to do that with another body. You're already hurt. If I drop you–"

"I'm going in first," Aleta said firmly. "I'm the lightest of all of us, and if I come in flaming, they are less likely to get off a shot." There was no arguing with her, as the small woman was resolute in her decision, and she had the tiny, lithe body of a dancer. Zephirine created a cushion of wind and held it down toward the ground until Aleta stepped on.

"All set?" the taller woman asked with trepidation, and she got a quick nod. "Up you go then," she whispered and gradually raised her palms to the sky, slowly lifting the air mass with a crouching, lightly glowing Aleta on board. Zephirine struggled a bit with keeping it level, but never faltered. Aleta was soon able to scramble onto the top of the wall that David Shepherd was already scouting along the base of for another way in.

There were shouts, and some blaster shots that scored the wall around her. Aleta lit up and she took a chance and leapt downward fully aflame, her fires crackling like an inferno.

And then the fight began in earnest!

~

Beneath the block and mortar fortified manor home of the late Georgie Rushman was a cellar area and a series of escape tunnels. Vixy knew them well, and was hauling a still groggy and battered but well trussed Alfie

Noble through a maze of them after relieving the guards on duty to join the firefight in the courtyard. Word of the boss' demise had not reached this lowest level of the compound yet, but the sounds of blaster fire and shouting from above had, and the men below were eager to join the battle. They were more than willing to leave the nearly senseless prisoner in the capable hands of Georgie's go-to gal, and had pounded up the steps, blasters in hand and scowls on their faces.

In the backpack slung over her shoulder, Jordyn within the Eye of Providence was being bumped along as she grunted and heaved, dragging the big, heavyset man by the rope that had bound him to the chair, refashioned into a harness of sorts. The stim she had injected had awakened him and he was at least compliant. He wasn't dead weight that way, and he could push himself along to help, but she'd kept Noble's wrists lashed to prevent him from fighting back, and they in turn were tied to a section fastened to his hobbled ankles. He was still half out of it but would eventually be able to stand and shuffle along, though he would not be capable of raising his arms, kicking her, or running off until she untied him.

Vixy was struggling to get him down a stairwell and around a sharp corner when the last scion of House Orion finally made his appearance.

There was a hissing noise as a beam of pure energy passed through the coarse weave of the fabric. Suddenly feeling the weight of the bag lessen, Vixy dropped Noble and spun around, blaster already drawn.

Jordyn stood before her in the darkness, the glow of the Eye of Providence bouncing up and down in his raised right hand while he pointed with a gloved and waggling left forefinger. His head was cocked sideways; a dark eyebrow arched over one brilliant aquamarine eye.

"You are a naughty, naughty girl! It's not nice to kill people and take away the things they covet you know," he said with a smirk.

Vixy never said anything, she just pulled the trigger.

The dark leather and lace clad clown with the mop of blond hair simply held up the glowing orb, and at the precise moment of impact it attracted and absorbed the blaster bolt, glowing white hot while it sapped all the energy from the weapon's power pack. "Is that all you know how to do—shoot at people you don't like?" he asked in a mocking voice.

She pulled the trigger in succession, but all she got was the whine of a drawn down battery. "What the hell are you supposed to be anyway?" she snarled, reaching for another weapon. It was dead as well.

"Jordyn Orion, formerly of House Orion, which is located in the Trapezium section of the nebula to be exact, though I doubt that means much to you. Let us just say that I am a bit of a star traveler. And as a Celestial Warden, I must warn you that you're on our watch list. Your patron divinity doesn't seem to think you're living up to his expectations. Blowing up a legendary being is not something to be done without careful consideration. Killing a nasty mortal is one thing, because they don't regenerate, but you don't want to be messing with upper level entities if you're not properly prepared. Things could get... ugly." He tilted his head the other way and raised the other eyebrow.

She was a bit spooked at how he had figured out what she was planning. As much of an atheist as she professed to be, Vixy Macall—like most of her weapon-for-hire ilk—was somewhat superstitious. She had seen and heard some strange things in her time, and knew all about the legend of the Harbormaster as well as other less pleasant folk tales. Rushman's insistence that it was all superstitious nonsense and he'd do as he damn well pleased was one of the things that had prompted her to take him out, before he stirred up things below waters that were best left alone unless you completely wiped them out.

Which was her plan all along.

"You drained my charge," she said uncertainly, tucking the useless blaster back into her holster and fingering something else.

"Oh, did I do that?" Jordyn said with mock concern as he held his hands over his heart, or where one would be if he had needed one. "I guess I forgot to mention that once I've reanimated it with my essence, it makes a fairly effective wave neutralizer." He twirled the Eye expertly on his fingertips and smiled with mischievous mirth. "Not that you've got a clue what I mean."

Faster than any human could move, he dodged sideways first one way and then another as she slung a pair of quad discs that as they flew, unfolded whirring razor arms that could slice through flesh and into bone. One struck the wall behind him and clattered to the stone floor, the other whirled around the corner and kept going until the buzz of its passage was lost in the echoing silence. Even the knife in her hand didn't daunt Jordyn, until she held it to Alfie Noble's throat.

"Back off Freak, or he dies for your stupidity," she warned Jordyn through gritted teeth. Demonic messenger or not, she was not giving up all she'd worked for without a fight!

Noble groaned and tried to heave himself more upright, his bruised and lumpy face a mask of pain. She shoved him before her and wrapped the knife arm around his chest, holding the blade flat against his thick

"Back off Freak, or he dies for your stupidity."

neck as he stiffened in her arms. "I keep this well-honed, by the way. One slice and it's all over."

"Tsk, tsk, tsk, you *so* disappoint me!" said Jordyn with an exaggerated sigh. "After all, if you did kill him, you'd lose your demolitions expert; so I doubt you have any intention of slicing him open," he added quietly, turning on all the persuasive charm he could muster, leaning forward with hands on hips. "Oh yes, I know all about your little plan; your subconscious thoughts were most voluble last night while you slept." He rolled the Eye back and forth across his arms and shoulders as he spoke, leaning to the right and left like a juggler, and noted with satisfaction that her eyes were riveted on the ritualistic motions. "I don't think we're really on opposite sides, dear girl; not when you consider the plight of the innocent people around you. No one in Yorkville liked what that ambitious cad you were working for was doing to the town. Rather brilliant coup actually, and likely a positive change of command. I thought it was rather shallow of you to take the old boy out the way you did, though he died happily I'd say. I suppose whatever works–"

This oddball was definitely addled, but then, most freaks were. "You're wasting my time," she said as the general alarm buzzer went off, and she began to drag a now somewhat awake and aware Noble down the tunnel. It was obvious that this Orion character no more wanted Noble dead than she did. "Big Georgie's goon squad will be down here soon, looking for me, and I have no plans of hanging around until they find us. Either get out of the way or give me a hand with this stumbling idiot so we don't all die here."

"Au contraire! With my team out there, they'll be busy for a while. But let's see if we can speed things along here," Jordyn said brightly, and he sprang forward and began to wave the Eye under Noble's nose and up and down his body, transferring energy. Then he stopped and studied it. "He'll be able to walk on his own now, but you have to untie his hands and feet if we're to make any progress," he added.

She slit the ropes, and Jordyn looked Alfie Noble in the eye. "Now be a good chap and come along peacefully, for I think we've something quite important for you to do here, and neither of us means you any further harm," he added with a wink and a pat on the shoulder.

Noble's lips were cracked and swollen, but he nodded wearily. "Water," he said thickly, and Vixy snorted.

"After we get out of this rat warren," she said, staying behind the two men in case she needed to pull the snub nosed ray gun tucked into an

ankle holster in her right boot. Soon the sounds of the firefight above receded as they passed through tunnels that lead them well into the area
below Down Sodom and on into the heart of the old city, where Vixy had
a crib with an arsenal that would take out all but a military attack. There,
the present situation would soon be resolved and then once Noble did his
part, she and Willy would get out of the city. She planned to head cross
country to somewhere neither of them were known, and they could start
over again.

Jordyn of course had other ideas about what Vixen Macall and her
rather able ward should be doing with their lives, but he paced along beside her and a stumbling Alfie Noble, and kept that information to himself.

For now anyway.

~

The sky lightened and the sun was rising below the ever roiling cloud
cover when a brightly burning Aleta Kalama dropped down onto the first
of the armed guards. He was standing idly on the catwalk perimeter inside the walled compound, watching someone below torturing a rat. He
never saw her leap off the wall and burst into flames before she turned him
black and crispy. His companions did though, and one of them managed
to snap off a blaster bolt at her before a whip of fire melted it into his flesh.
He howled in agony and fell to his knees clutching his contorted and useless arm as the guy behind him lifted a pulse rifle to fire over him at Aleta.

David Shepherd pounded forward from the shadows down the catwalk
to tackle him. He leapt and took the rifleman square in the back and they
both went down. Groaning with the pain of his fractured ribs, Shepherd
still managed to roll against the wall, but the unfortunate guard upended
with the weight of the heavy weapon. He let go of the gun and clawed for
the rail as he tumbled over the side. The shot went wild, blowing a hole in
the concrete above Davey, who ducked and covered as he was spattered
with dust and pelted with shards. The man he had jumped screamed in
terror as he lost his tenuous grip and fell backwards to hit head first onto
the pavement below. A few spasmodic jerks and it was all over.

Shepherd grabbed the rifle as soon as he regained his feet. He finished
off the man with the mangled arm with a point blank shot to the temple
even before his own ears stopped ringing. Waving to Aleta as she headed
for the nearest stairs down, he raced along the catwalk looking for someone else to take out.

A lightly armed man in the yard fired at Aleta and then ran back inside shouting a warning. The shot gazed her shoulder, and she jumped sideways and went down rolling, losing her flames for a moment. More than one blaster bolt crackled forth from the walls above, but she was quick on her feet, up and running while dodging, and the hand weapon range wasn't as good as the more expensive and less reliable pulse rifles that only a few of the catwalk guards carried.

Aleta was headed for the big building in the center of the compound when there was the deafening sound of a klaxon and armed men poured out into the courtyard from several different directions. Another shot caught her in the back, far enough out of range not to do any more than knock her breathlessly to her knees, but once again her fire went out.

Gasping to refill her lungs, she was somewhat dazed, and had to fight to regain her feet again, let alone find the energy to light up. The night had been long. Aleta was exhausted, and shots were coming from all around. Trying not to become any more of a target, she drunkenly zigzagged around the building and dove under the cover of a nearby armored coach.

Someone lobbed a gas canister at her, and fortunately Aleta saw it roll by. She kicked it back into the yard and scrambled out the far end, only to face down two more men coming straight at her. David Shepherd took out one of them, but he couldn't get the other without endangering Aleta. He ran down the walkway, angling to get a better shot, and began taking fire. Stuck defending his own position, he couldn't see through the concrete dust and rock splinters around him as bolt after bolt hit where he had just been.

~

Still unsure of her fighting abilities, Zephirine had sailed up and now crouched low atop one of the abandoned guard towers, looking for an opportunity to join the fray without making herself a floating target. She saw Aleta was pinned down and in trouble. David had problems of his own, and that made up her mind. All the attention was focused on her companions now.

Jumping down safely with the help of a buoying air current, she landed lightly on the catwalk. Raising her arms and circling them counter-wise, she blew up a loose whirlwind and pointed down until it encircled Aleta, cutting her off from her attackers. Once her companion regained control of her powers, Zephirine pulled it off her and tightened the vortex, sending it spinning wildly amongst the men chasing Aleta. The dust devil twisted violently, scouring sand and grit from the courtyard into their faces. With Zephirine guiding it from above, it was impossible for the attacking men to see the flaming woman as she raced by, torching one after another with broiling blasts while lobbing fireballs.

Up on the wall, the pulse rifle pounded over and over as a cursing David Shepherd began to pick off his share of the well spooked and quickly scattering guards.

The defenders cleared for the moment, Zephirine used that opportunity to leap into the air, pulling the billowing winds below her as she rode the dying cone to the ground. She bounced down and landed next to a writhing, grimacing burn victim. She blew him into another man, who was desperately trying to stand up on legs that refused to recover from the nerve damage of a dead-on pulse hit. They both smacked a nearby wall rather abruptly and lay still.

"You're hurt!" Zephirine said with concern, seeing the strip of seared flesh beneath the burned away shoulder of Aleta's shirt. Her sister-in-arms had stopped against a wall for a breather, letting her flames die down, though her dark eyes kept scanning the area for more assailants.

"Don't worry about me, it's just a thin score," Aleta insisted tiredly as Zephirine came up to her. "Go get Alfie. David and I will mop up out here," she added as she lit up and turned to guard the entranceway for them.

Zephirine didn't argue. She was much better at the search and rescue stuff than fighting anyway. While Aleta ran helter-skelter amongst the stumbling and nearly blinded thugs that Shepherd hadn't already knocked down, torching one after another with long strands of red hot flames, the mistress of winds stalked calmly into the building. She ignored the screeching and shrieking behind her, for her attention was on one thing alone—where were they holding Alfred Noble?

The place was opulent beyond anything she had seen in many a cycle, and the riches displayed there would have supported many a poor household in Yorkville for the year. Much of it was imported, so this Rushman character had long been skimming cargoes and keeping the best for himself. The rest had obviously bought him the small army he had deployed outside, for no one seemed to remain in the household but a few domestic servants and they mostly ran when the saw the tall, grim, hazel-eyed woman with the ever present wind that whistled through her long dark overcoat and mussed brown hair.

David Shepherd had also gained entrance to the building and came up alongside her as she prowled deeper into the now quiet early morning residence. "Quite the palace this bloke 'as," he quipped, pointing at bits and pieces of shiny old machinery and mechs, and rarities like medical supplies and prewar electronic devices. "I take it no one e'er comes in 'ere, or 'is bleedin' collection woulda been burgled long ago."

"David… excess like this goes well beyond simple collecting," she said with a quizzical expression. "This is an obsession. He wants something bigger in this world. He'd have to have ambitious plans to hold on to all this precious stuff for so long, because it's only worth what you can get in trade. There are things in here that could support you and me for the rest of our lives, with the right buyer."

"Ye've done a fair bit of trading in yer time I take it," he said appreciatively, for the longtime seaman also knew the value of many of the items they were passing. He could tell some of them had been recovered below the lapping waves, for they bore the unmistakable signs of having once been waterlogged. Of those, most were original to Columbiana, and that meant they had likely been retrieved from flooded areas of the old city below.

"Enough bartering to know a sizable fortune when I see it," she said with consternation. "But the base of my orrery isn't here. And where is Alfie?"

Shepherd clicked his tongue over the first part. "Likely they 'ave 'im locked up somewhere safe. Let's find us someone to talk to, and get to the bottom o' this blasted mess." He brandished the pulse rifle for effect. "With the drubbing you ladies been givin' 'is pack of thugs, this piece alone should get an audience with the kingpin—if 'e ain't already run off like a scared cabin boy."

It was not long before they cornered a quailing chambermaid and found out the ugly truth: Big Georgie Rushman had been found dead in his bed, and the battered man who'd been hauled down to the wine cellar had disappeared with Rushman's second in command and favorite rogue for hire, Vixen Macall. Willy's so-called aunt had gotten to Alfred Noble before they had, and so the entire firefight had been for naught.

"You know, I hate this damned town!" Aleta said after they exited the building and told her the news. The sun was well up, the compound was strewn with dead and burnt corpses, and other than having secured Zephirine's orrery, they were no farther ahead than they had been when they entered the fight.

"Not my favorite place either," Zephirine, admitted. "And just where in Hades' Shades is Jordyn?"

The Harbormaster Awakens!

Willy Teller probably would have been fine if he had been content to stay trussed to the seaward end of the rotted old dock. Eventually someone would have come by in a boat and cut him loose. But he was a stubborn, impulsive young man; and he and Vixy were about to lose a fortune. No way was he letting that happen!

Shepherd had been in a hurry to tie Willy up, and while *Solstice*'s new captain was angry with the young man, he was not particularly cruel by nature. With his longtime sailor's knowledge of ropes and knots, he made the restraints holding the protesting youngster adequately tight, but not enough to cut off his circulation. Tired, battered, and in a hurry to get back to the ladies and do some strategic planning for their raid, David hadn't noticed that Willy had taken a big lung full of air and had tensed his shoulders and arms enough to make the rope a bit slacker than it should be once he relaxed and exhaled. As soon as the three of them were out of earshot and the noise of a firefight at Big Georgie's place had started up, the enterprising lad wiggled and shimmied until he could at least get his hands relatively free.

Limber and lithe, Willy exhaled deeply to loosen the bonds further. That gave him enough slack so he could crouch down, painfully scraping his back on the rough wood while trying to pull a slender little strip of metal from his boot. It was something that he often used as a lock-pick, but at that point he had the idea of sawing it back and forth across the surface of the rope that bound his arms. He was in the midst of a second try to reach it when he heard the piling he was tied to begin to crack.

Breaking the piling off and sliding out of the coils would be a much faster way to get free. Waggling himself from side to side made the top of the wooden post above him lean first this way and that. His hope was that it would shear off above the decking, but it soon became evident that was not the case.

With a final groan and crack, the piling broke away well below the base of the dock. It tipped him sideways over the edge, and Willy Macall landed with a tremendous splash, still lashed tight and floating out into the deep water of the harbor on the punky old log.

The gag at least was wet enough to sag free. He spit it out and began to yell, though no one was nearby to hear him. He was too far out of the shipping lanes and the local fishermen were already headed out to sea for the day. The rope soon became saturated and tightened, and his frantic attempts to set himself free kept ducking him under. After a while he was exhausted, and just drifted along with the lapping waves, hoping to be seen by a boat he could hail to pull him in.

Unfortunately, it was not a boat that noticed him first. An ominous bump on the bottom end of the piling rolled him sideways to the left. With rising panic, he saw a wedge shaped fin cutting toward him, with the dark mass of a large, streamlined body beneath it.

It was a shark!

Another bump and the poke of a snout against his boot spun him the other way. Three more sharks were coming in from the right!

The sharks that prowled New Brooklyn Harbor were large, with a fierce and sinister reputation as man eaters. Willy frantically tried to think what he should do. He'd always heard sharks didn't eat dead meat without blood to scent, but the bodies that floated out to sea made a lie of that. The big fierce ones always hung around the drowned city, and he was out in the channel between the arms of that. There wasn't a boat in his area, as they all tended to skirt the sunken islands, and he floated too low in the water to be seen from any distance. He was as good as dead, for whether he struggled or not, the sharks were starting to take nips at the log piling and getting close to him, teeth snagging and tearing his clothing. As soon as one of them drew blood, it was all over.

"Well, I'm not going down without a fight!" he declared, smacking a heel into a wedge shaped head and feeling the creature recoil. A tooth had pierced the leather though, and the telltale sting of salt in a cut told him the time of attack was almost upon him. As the sharks closed in, surging at him, he shut his eyes, and breathed a bit of a prayer his bold pirating Da had taught him, hoping the gods of sea and foam at least were listening, and the blackness of oblivion would come on him fast, before he knew the agony of being rent apart by many sets of sharp, serrated teeth.

~

Something out in the depths of the cold water sensed a fervent prayer to die with dignity, and it was stirred. A great head lifted, a body moved, and bulging, cold silvery eyes slowly opened and blinked. A scent came through the water, pale and thin, but even so thickly tainted with the fear stench of mankind, it bore an unmistakable hint of the off-world mermen. It was worth investigating, to see which of the foolish humans was consorting with the water demons from another age. Atlantis would not rise again, not here, not in this now peaceful place.

A huge form shot out of the bell-like cave formed from the crumpled verdigris skirt of what was once a symbol of freedom for the masses, leaving a few large sharks circling its lair as guardians of the treasure hidden deep within. A behemoth monster of the primordial world swam rapidly toward the part of the local shoreline where some other very excited sharks were toying with what appeared to be a corpse lashed to a log.

Another sacrifice? Or something far more intriguing? He would find out soon.

Fists the size of the casks of rum the boatmen tossed into the bay to honor the Unknowable Deep Ones plowed into shark bodies right and left, batting them out of the way. They were no more than unruly pets, and when one of them slipped back past the Harbormaster, he grabbed it roughly by the tail and slung it far away. It hit the underwater part of a building hard enough to stun it, drawing blood; and all others that were not too battered and bruised to take advantage of the situation began to cannibalize their hapless brethren. Sharp white teeth tore great chunks of bloody meat free, and swam off before another dodged in to take away the prize. In moments the water around the injured shark was churning red and it was quickly reduced to a quivering bit of flesh and bone that settled to the bottom.

Except for small, superficial wounds, none had harmed the land-walking child of mankind. But he was half drowned and in shock, so he did not even struggle when the large, long clawed fingers with expandable webbing between them lifted him and the piling he was lashed to free of the water.

~

They searched Big Georgie's compound thoroughly but no one was able to locate Alfred Noble. Most of the staff left were poorly paid domestic help or carriage drivers, and all were eager to leave with whatever items they could haul off. The place would be completely looted by the end of the day.

"Ah just let 'em go," Shepherd said to Aleta as she made as if to give chase to a maid lugging boxes of silver plate. "He likely owes 'em more'n that for all the trouble he caused here."

"We can't just leave the place to be pillaged!" Zephirine said with a huge frown. She never had approved of stealing from the dead.

"Yorkville will sort itself out over time, Missy Zee," he reassured her as they left the grounds of his compound. "Used to be a nice little port town afore Georgie Rushman took over. These be good, hard working folks for the most part. They'll choose someone less of a tyrant to be the law."

"Why did they let this racketeer take over in the first place?" Zephirine asked with a furrowed brow.

"The usual reasons. Rushman made speeches with big promises and 'e seemed to be able to keep the riffraff out. I don't think 'e showed his true colors 'til there was no one left to oppose 'im. And 'e always was smooth with words when it suited 'im," he added, remembering how things were in his youth.

"People need someone to lead them. Someone to believe in," Aleta added as they made their way back down toward the old docks. The couple of looters they came across looked frightened and ran off as they approached. "Word gets around fast," she added with a sigh.

"Always does in these small towns," Shepherd said in a distracted tone. They were within sight of the abandoned dock where he had left the boy, but Willy was missing, as well as the piling he'd been tied to.

The burly little man swore under his breath. "That slippery little brat 'as more lives than a cat!" he said with frustration.

"Well, at least he didn't get my orrery this time," Zephirine said with relief as she retrieved it from under the rotten boat. "But what do we do now?"

"We need to find Jordyn," Aleta said firmly. "He can help us locate Alfie."

~

Aleta, Zephirine, and David split up. Aleta and Shepherd set out in different directions in the early morning light of the new day to search for Jordyn, while Zephirine took her orrery, still disguised as old driftwood, and hastened back across town to hide it amongst her things once more.

She hustled along the late awakening streets of the back edge of town, weaving through the bleary-eyed crowd. Trying to look casual at the same time she was keeping an eye open for danger as well as signs of Alfred Noble or Jordyn, her fatigue was getting the best of her. While attempting to step over the long legs of a sprawling drunk who was sleeping it off in the alley, Zephirine was in the midst of a cavernous yawn when she stumbled and bumped into a curvaceous woman armed with a blaster in a hip holster.

"Watch where you're going," the woman said gruffly, shoving past her and hurrying on her way.

Zephirine turned to retort when she noticed that walking well ahead of the armed woman was a smugly smirking Jordyn Orion hauling along a stumbling and battered Alfie Noble. "Hey, those are my friends!" she shouted, stomping up from behind.

As Zephirine approached the trio, the suspicious woman with the blaster dropped away from Noble and Jordyn, and drew a bead on her. "They're my business now, so get lost," she warned.

Zephirine tucked the disguised orrery under under one arm while raising the other one palm outwards and nonchalantly blew Vixen Macall onto her backside.

"Nicely done!" said Jordyn with a big, ingratiating smile. "You didn't even hesitate." He picked up the blaster, and handed it to Alfie Noble, who had enough sense left in him to hold it steady on the very dangerous woman who had abducted him. "I love it when the autonomic response kicks in and you don't have to think twice before defending yourself and those around you. I told you that you would make a fine team member My Dear," he added enthusiastically.

Zephirine had seen enough fighting for one day. She was tired beyond belief, very frustrated with the entire situation, and in no mood for happy banter. Her answer was a string of profanity worthy of a dockworker. Having gotten that off her chest, she stood glowering at Jordyn while continuing to press Vixy flat with a gale force wind pinpoint directed to keep the struggling woman from being able to get to her feet.

"Was that outburst really necessary?" Jordyn asked her with an arched eyebrow and hands on hips. "Some of that is physically impossible anyway. At least... I think it is," he added with a quizzical expression half between intrigued and disturbed at her crudity.

"Well, you earned it!" Zephirine replied emphatically. "While you were gadding about town, we've just been having one battle after another tonight. So I've about had it with the hero business!" she added, moving closer to narrow the focus of the wind, which allowed Jordyn and a very slow moving and groaning Alfie Noble to frisk the woman she had pinned to the ground, relieving her of a few other concealed weapons. Several onlookers hurried by, trying not to see some female laying in the gutter being accosted by a big man and a 'heeshee' while another woman stood by cussing them out. Gang business was not their concern anyway. "So where in hell have you been Jordyn?" she demanded bluntly, her patience about gone.

He blinked at her tone, looking rather shocked. "Why... I've been out saving the world of course!" he said a bit apologetically. "Same as you. Oh, and I found us another team member, a Finnman who swims like a fish–"

"Yeah, we met him. He returned something of mine that was lost," she said, patting the disguised orrery under one arm.

Jordyn brightened at that one, his smile wide and all dimples. "Then you already know what an asset Roan will be to us." He leaned in conspiratorially. "Do you think it's wise to walk around openly with that device?" He indicated what to the others appeared to be a piece of driftwood under her arm. "It's infinitely valuable, and if we find the missing part, rather powerful as well! Someone might try to steal it."

"Someone already tried—twice," she snapped in a dry, exasperated tone, wondering how he knew what it was. "And the little monster got away from us. In the meantime, we basically took out the entire underworld here to save Alfie and all for naught, because you're walking around with blasted Noble hanging on your arm like nothing happened!" Her voice went up until she was shouting, and a crowd had started to gather.

"Zephirine dear, there's nothing that's done for no good reason," Jordyn said soothingly, "and at the end of this, you'll realize that. If you've already dismantled the crime element, then Yorkville will be a far better place to live. Of course, some other things have happened that you would not be privy to, and they need explaining; but not right now," he added as a bell in the harbor began to ring and was answered by ships' horns and other bells around the town. "I think we have a rather larger problem on our hands. You'd better go secure that little surprise of yours somewhere safely, because someone else wants it as badly as you do, if not more so. And *he* doesn't take 'no' for an answer," Jordyn added, gesturing down toward the shore.

They all turned to look in the direction Jordyn was indicating. Rising from the sea, with water pouring off a silvery green torso, was one of the ancient horrors of the deep. It blocked the harbor exit, arms out, tail churning the waves to foam beneath it. When it opened its mouth, it roared in defiance, and reached out to capsize a small boat trying to slip by.

"What is *that*?" Zephirine asked with rising concern. Her concentration broken, she abruptly let go of the wind that was pinning Vixy Macall down.

"An old acquaintance of my family," Jordyn said slowly and with distaste. "I should have known that anywhere the Atlanteans feared to invade, one of the more proactive of the Lords of the Deep would be resident. That is Dagon, and while he hates the merfolk, he's not particularly fond of humans either. I think you had better get that item out of here now Dear, before we lose it. I'll get a team together down by the docks. The *Solstice* may have to sail today…"

His voice trailed off, as Jordyn headed resolutely through the open mouthed crowd watching the drama in the harbor. He stopped abruptly and began waving frantically to someone they couldn't yet see.

Zephirine turned to Alfie Noble, who still had the blaster. "Can you handle her on your own?"she asked quietly.

"I'll manage," he answered, yanking a breathless and no longer struggling Vixen Macall to her feet, while keeping her covered with her own weapon. He twisted an arm behind her back. "I got a feeling you're going to need all the firepower we've got anyway."

"We might! I've got to go put something away, but I'll be back. In the meantime, get everyone you can find who can fight or crew a ship down to the shore dock with Jordyn. Looks like we're going out to parley or something." She turned to go but stopped when she saw some familiar faces coming through the throng, and headed down the street toward them. Aleta and David Shepherd had reunited and they were hurrying along at Jordyn's side, the small, dark woman's tired eyes backlit with mixture of relief, consternation, and concern.

"You certainly made yourself scarce last night," Aleta said accusingly to her mentor.

"I had business to attend to," Jordyn answered in a peevish tone, but never took his eyes off the scene across the harbor. Dagon had not announced his presence until that moment, and while Jordyn had sensed that one of the elder Lords of the Deep was somewhere nearby, he had hoped for someone more benign and easier to reason with, like Triton or Proteus. Dagon was more demonic than godlike, and while he remained relatively tractable when undisturbed, he was no longer pretending to be benevolent. It had generally been his nature to subjugate and torment mankind, and he often demanded tribute or sacrifices.

"I think we have a very big problem on our hands," Jordyn said without enthusiasm.

Aleta's angry glare at him dimmed and she gave a troubled sigh and a shake of her tousled hair as she glanced out to sea. "It never ends, does it?" she said quietly, as he slipped an arm around her shoulders.

"No, not in this age, I fear," he answered quietly.

～

"Alfie lad, ye be alive!" David Shepherd said with a broad smile, clapping his mate on the shoulder, and getting a wince in response. He looked over the woman Noble was holding a blaster on, wondering what her part in this was.

Alfred Noble cleared his throat. "Aye, I'll live, but I could do with a drink and some rest," the battered man said with a one-eyed squint. "What in hell's goin' on out there though?" He gestured toward the harbor.

Shepherd's look was grim. "A bad business this is! The boatmen say they can't get in or out. The 'arbormaster has risen, and 'e insists 'e must 'ave some otherworld device," David Shepherd told them, eyeing Zephirine significantly as he did. "No one seems to have a clue what the old beastie means, but 'e 'as that lad Willy Teller, and means to tear 'im apart if we don' give it to him." He watched the woman as he said that, getting the reaction he expected.

"Let me go!" Vixy insisted, yanking herself free of Alfred Noble. "That's Walter Teller's kid; his father was my partner, and my best friend!" Having distracted Alfie, she grabbed the blaster from him in one smooth motion. She pointed the weapon at first one then another of them, but there was no way to cover them all as she backed away.

"Oh, now this is interesting," Jordyn said with a tilt of his head as he drew the Eye of Providence from his shirt in case the desperate woman decided to fire. "You seem to have at least one soft spot in that cold, mercenary heart. Since you seem to want your protégé back in one piece, it would be best if we all worked together."

"All I want is the kid, you can have the rest," she said levelly, and there was fear in her eyes for the first time. All the things that Vixy had put up with those long months with Georgie Rushman had been to give the boy a better life than his father had known, somewhere else besides on the sea. And now, the entire situation was blowing up in her face.

"Then put the blasted weapon down, and we'll do what we can for him," Aleta said quietly, as she stepped up with a hand out, though the fire backlighting her eyes was a warning not to do anything stupid. Vixy looked at her a long moment, and there was confusion on her face, but her hand holding the blaster wavered and then dropped to her side.

"There is hope for you yet, Mistress Macall. Or should I say, Lady Macbeth?" Jordyn added with a pointed look at her.

"There are no titles like that in this age! But... how did you know that?" she asked Jordyn in a flabbergasted tone as she holstered her weapon, which she already knew was useless against the Eye. Few would have made the connection that her line had changed names to avoid the stain of that all-too-powerful, but ultimately insane ancestress.

He presented the Eye, turning it from side to side. "I know everything I need to know," he said with a smug smile. "Your helix signature is readable in here, and it matches hers at key points. While you're an equally ambitious and ruthless woman, we wouldn't want you to follow too closely in her footsteps, because her end was far less desirable. I think you can channel that drive to succeed in more positive ways, so that you can be a boon to this community. But right now we have bigger issues than who killed whom in a former life."

He lowered the Eye, dropping it back into his shirt and spread his hands apart to make a point. "Ladies and gentlemen, I propose a truce, because we all have a vested interest in not seeing this town starved out and innocent people killed off in a protracted siege. We can use all the good fighters we can get, because Dagon is ever a formidable foe, and he's not exactly altruistic toward humanity. In fact, he's rather bloodthirsty at his best, and it will take all our skills and plenty of luck to keep this from becoming a massacre. But first of all, Zephirine my dear, *please* make sure you secure that item well inland and then meet us down at the shoreline. I've got some planning to do. It's going to be an interesting day."

"Always something," Zephirine said tiredly as she scurried off again. Jordyn left Vixen Macall with Alfred Noble and David Shepherd while he and a very tired looking Aleta Kalama headed back down toward the sea. As they passed through, the crowd parted in deference, for word had gotten around Yorkville that Big Georgie Rushman and all his goons had perished at the hands of these heroic strangers from across the ocean.

~

The sea boiled around him and there was the feeling of being carried just above the surface. Willy Teller wasn't sure if he was already dead or just delirious with pain and dreaming all of it as he coughed and sputtered, retching and gagging out the seawater being pressed from his lungs. He eventually opened his eyes, and then immediately wished he hadn't.

No wonder the sharks had all backed off as he had been yanked under and began to drown! His heart was now sick with fear as he was carried out to sea into the gray and rose light of dawn by something out of nightmares and legends.

He lowered the Eye, dropping it back into his shirt...

A head and neck loomed above him, and Willy watched helplessly as he was raised on high. A hideous beast of the deep peered down at him. Large fish eyes, alien and inhuman, but filled with malevolent intelligence, studied him from an iridescent scaled face more akin to sea life than it was humanoid. The mouth gaped open, showing a double row of thin, dagger length, back-curving teeth.

"Good, you have fear! Fear is strong motivator. So where is star locator, manchild?" demanded a deep and heavily accented voice with the sound of bubbling water garbling the speech. As the coldly appraising, impersonal stare captivated the quaking young man, a great heavy body that ended in a long serpentine tail lashed impatiently beneath the waves. *"Quick, tell me now and death will be merciful. Not tell and Dagon bites off small parts one at a time until you beg to die!"*

"I d-don't know! The-the friends of Orion took it from me." It was mostly true anyway and the best thing Willy could think to say.

The smile was bitter, and showed far too many long, curved teeth as the behemoth nodded. *"O-ri-on..."* he dragged out the name deliberately and with distaste as the great eyes glinted coldly. *"That House name I know. His smell I know!"* Something akin to a sneer came over the face. *"Always meddling in the affairs of humans. All Orion ancestors were the same. They all died out, and this one will too. No matter; Orion House is always soft-hearted with mortals. He will trade for your life, and I will have my boon!"* He gnashed his teeth, lifting the lad to his lips, breathing out the stink and slime of ages of sea life before he sniffed at the boy again. Willy fainted, feeling he was going to die for certain this time.

The human did still smell faintly of the offworld star locator. The sea god's laughter was loud, long, hollow, and mirthless. His lengthy and well muscled arms were the size of the big forest trees that had stood tall and proud before the wars, his grasping webbed digits were tipped with huge, strong claws like swords. Those claws formed a cage around Willy Teller as he bore the boy still trussed to a water soaked log well out to sea. The sea god's sinuously powerful body was propelled along by a length of finny tail as Lord Dagon, the serpent god, made off with his bargaining chip, a mortal who smelled faintly of the missing travel device belonging to the renegade Atlanteans.

Those star traveling merfolk used to worship him when they first came to Earth, but did no longer. Now they only wanted his death at the end of their tridents, as Dagon had thwarted their plans to capture and claim this water planet as their own. He had guarded and kept from them the abandoned star chart base of their guidance device for many cycles since the great wars, after retrieving it from the drowned city. His presence in New Brooklyn Harbor held the Atlanteans at bay, and that was how Dagon preferred it, lest the other part be found and the sections reunited.

Yet now that it had been located, there was a great danger to this small world he had grown fond of. For if the Atlanteans possessed it in entirety, they would raise the island continent they had built for themselves long ago and reopen their fortress again. If they activated the portal into space and time that was within the sunken city, they would bring in the rest of their kind. Earth would be overrun in no time, hastening yet another Armageddon. That instrument could not be left in the hands of mortals, for they were too foolish to realize its worth, and Dagon would kill every human and demigod he had to in order to prevent that.

But humans were such sentimental creatures. If they still had the rest of the world spinner hidden away someplace and did not realize its potential, they might make an offering of it to get one of their pitiful sons back. If not, well… they were all good eating, even this small and bony one, and he'd be the first to die for their folly. A human a day would be killed right in plain sight, in their own harbor, a single screeching, quivering bite at a time.

Orion's son would not let that happen. He loved the mortals too well. Orion would bring forth the rest of the device. That Dagon was certain of.

He stowed the limp and still trussed boy on a rocky prominence that stayed dry above the lapping waves, even at the highest tide. The sunken land around it was so shallow below the surface, no ship dared approach, and the sharks that circled it made swimming away all but impossible. Dagon turned back and headed toward the shore town again. Blocking the outlet to the sea, he rose to his highest in the water, braced by his great tail lashed around part of an underwater building. Arms crossed on plated chest, he glared at the harbor balefully, waiting for the next group of boats leaving their slips to notice him before thundering in a great cavernous voice.

"Who has the star locator? Where is Orion? Bring it to me, son of the stars, or I will kill this mortal and many more until I have it. Dagon has spoken!"

Even the nearby sharks went to the depths and quivered at the wrath of the serpent god of the sea.

Inspired To Lead and To Serve

On his own island, just outside the harbor, Roan watched and wondered what to do. There was no way to get close to the boy, not with Dagon nearby, as he kept the only clear channel in and out of New Brooklyn Harbor blockaded. But the behemoth guardian of the deep water was occupied with the humans and not paying much attention to what was going on below, and there were always ways through the sunken buildings that a boat could never navigate but a stealthy sea creature might.

He couldn't rescue the little thief, but he might be able to defuse the situation. Dagon wanted the offworld device mainly to keep it out of the hands of his rivals for supremacy. If the Orion Numen and his heroic team took it inland, there should be no further problems from it.

Of course, Roan knew that if he meddled in the affairs of the Serpent God, there would be no peace for him in the ocean around New Brooklyn, and he would have to move on. But he was ready for that; to go forth with this group of landwalker individuals who wanted to save Earth from Armageddon once again. That meant leaving the sea behind, which would not be easy. Still, neither would facing endless cycles of raw fish and bone chilling winter surf until he was too old to hunt for himself any longer. The future Jordyn Orion had proposed sounded far more enticing than spending the rest of his days alone, now that the dolphin Free—his only local friend—had joined a pod and had a new life of her own out at sea.

Roan knew what most others did not. The Great One had the star chart base of the orrery secured within his cavernous resting place deep beneath the waves. With both parts of that device reunited and back in working order, Dagon planned to use it so that he could find a way back to his former age of glory, when all mankind trembled at his name and Atlantis was virtually unknown. Once there and with his memory intact, the Elder God could alter events enough that he remained in power over humanity. The fish people who had designed it had used it for other purposes the half selkie didn't completely understand, though it was rumored to be able to locate items lost in time and space, including some sort of island dwelling that had long ago sunk beneath the waves. There was no doubt that it was something the displaced merfolk coveted very much, so much so that their females mesmerized nearby ships to their doom to search cargoes for it. The base alone called continually to them, and if not for the fierce guardian beneath the waves, they would have laid waste long ago to Yorkville and everything around it in their haste to have it.

And now that the rest had been found, they would be doubly eager to have it. Something had to be done; for once it all rested in Dagon's treasure hoard, there would be no peace in the world. The fish people would be merciless in their attempts to obtain it. Dagon would fight back just as furiously, and the humans would only be in the way. There would be war on the seas again, and all would suffer.

Peace was something even the despised and reviled son of a selkie desired more than anything else in his life, for he had seen enough upheaval and warfare, greed and mistrust, to last him a lifetime.

Roan moved cautiously about at a half crouch, positioning himself on the seaward part of his little rocky spit so as not to be noticed when he left. The Numen Orion had told him that sometimes you had to do courageous things without expecting to be rewarded, or even lauded, just because they were the right things to do. Certainly the desirable and very brave ladies who traveled with Jordyn had not hesitated to pitch in, and the Numen had related that while they each had special talents, they were not much more battle savvy than Roan himself. They simply used whatever resources and skills they had acquired in ways that they knew and understood, and fought together for a common cause. Somehow, that seemed to be good enough.

There was only one way to end this stalemate, and perhaps save some lives in the process, but it would take a lot of bravado and some help from friends. If even a half-selkie Finnman could make a difference, perhaps the world would become a bit better place, and maybe, he might find a permanent home within it.

Roan dove into the water, swimming out and away from the enraged Harbormaster. Once safely at sea, he began long range calling to Free and her pod in their own language of clicks and whistles, summoning his small cetacean friends to assist him in getting into Dagon's lair and retrieving the one item the serpent god feared most falling into the wrong hands.

~

Jordyn, Aleta, and David Shepherd had spent a short time catching up on what had transpired overnight while Alfred and Vixy went off to secure some powder kegs and blasting materials from Georgie Rushman's hidden supplies. All that would be hauled aboard *Solstice*, which was still at sea dock, being refitted and repaired. They would have to charter a row-boat to take them out to the big ship, which was still well off land, though it was at least within the harbor.

"What are *we* going to do?" Aleta asked Jordyn as they stood on the end of the biggest mainland dock, her skin already glowing brightly.

"What we always do," he replied smoothly while watching Dagon close-ly with narrowed aquamarine eyes, as the serpent god was threatening another boat trying to slip past him. "We'll do what we're best at, and deal with it."

"How?" she asked with a tired sounding voice. "We can't exactly hand Zephirine's astro-thingy over to that overgrown shipworm."

Jordyn smiled at her nautical reference. For a woman who had never even seen the sea before her latest adventures, she was picking up mari-time terms fairly well.

"Of course we won't do that! That's far larger a treasure than you could ever imagine! And quite useful to us too, I might add. For now I will go bargain for young William Teller's life. You should join Masters Noble and Shepherd when they sail, for I believe they will have some use for your abilities."

"And what about Zephirine?" she asked, hustling to catch up with his hopping stride as he hurried down to the dock, looking for a launching point as he pulled the Eye of Providence free of his shirt once more.

"Tell her to stay out of the water, she smells too strongly of Atlantis. I'm sure she'll find something interesting to do on shore with that wind of hers," he called back before disappearing into the Eye and flying across the harbor to look over the situation. He spotted Willy lashed to a log on a small rocky island, noting there was a sunken building's protruding top near enough to address Dagon in person. There was no sign of the Finnman though, and that was a disappointment. He headed out to the sea dock, dropping out of the Eye aboard *Solstice*.

"Fine! I'll just go light more things on fire," Aleta grumbled as she turned back the way she came to look for David Shepherd, who was sup-posed to be arranging transportation out to *Solstice*.

⁓

What Finnman wants of us? Free asked once she and her pod swam in. The other dolphins were uneasily circling a bobbing Roan and a paddling Free in the open water. They were sending clicks and whistles back and forth amongst themselves, chattering about the local sea god having risen in anger.

"I need help getting into the Harbormaster's lair," he told her in her own language. "He has big sharks down there I can't fight off. If you can distract them long enough for me to slip in and out, I think I can take away the thing he guards and make the sea safer for all."

That dangerous! Free answered, and she whistled shrilly in fear. *Big One not like us to come close and touch his things. He might hunt us down. Kill us for food.* Most of her pod chattered nervously about such a foolish idea, for while sharks could be evaded, Dagon was a formidable enemy.

"I know, but I need you to be brave for me, so that my friends and I can do something important that makes the world better for all," Roan answered quietly. "It is the last favor I will ask of you Free. Then you can go off to be with your pod and I will go off with mine." Roan realized at that moment he meant it, that he really wanted to be part of that specialized team the Numen Orion had asked him to join. Roan found that he wanted to do big, important things too, and help clear the clouds from minds and hearts as well as the ever roiling skies.

Some of the others chattered excitedly, advising Free to refuse, but she circled Roan, clicking, whining, and whistling in a troubled tone. *I owe Finnman my life,* she told them. *Finnman brave! Finnman chewed nets loose before I drowned. Breathe again good. I go with Finnman then. Those who join me, come fight with us. Those who not, I hope to live and hunt with again.* She was adamant, and swam round and round Roan, whistling long and shrill.

A large, scarred male dolphin swam up, obviously the leader of the pod. He stared at Roan as he circled, clicking angrily. *Why you make more trouble for us, Finnman? We swim out to deeps where hunting is good, and juicy fish are easy to find. But fish people hunt us. Monsters killing us. We come to shore, and humans want to hunt us. Where do we find peace in this water? Not here. Not there. No place is safe long, so we go now.*

He swam off, and the others began to follow, but Roan swam just as fast, and swirled around the scarred one, getting in his face.

"If we don't intervene, the god will kill the humans, and then more of them will come to fight back, and other gods will get involved. There will be war again. More bombs and mines," Roan insisted, reminding Free as well as showing others in shared mental images of what happens when humans retaliate. "The sky will rain fire, and the water will burn. The fish will go away, and we will be hunted down because we are of the sea too.

You can swim away, and so can I, but the humans cannot use deep water to dive into and breathe long. They will have to stay and fight, and they will use bad things that burn skin and eyes, and all will suffer. If we stop that now, all will live free, and more juicy fish will come back. Maybe the fish folk will go away in time. Help me and I promise things will become better around here, with calmer water to swim in. I will tell the humans that you helped, and they will not hunt you anymore."

That was a long shot promise, but Roan knew that with Jordyn Orion's influence, it might be doable.

Safe shores good. Fishing good. No hunting us good, Free insisted, projecting an image of dolphin guided ships coming into the harbor without nets to tangle them or seal gunners firing. *Big water is full of monsters now, even with no wars. I like Finnman's world better! I fight with him!*

I fight too! A small male said. *I want stay here. Not swim far and away all time. I want good life. Plenty fish. Not eaters killing my mates and young!*

The pod was getting excited, swimming round and round, chattering and jumping with the idea. Often caught between the dangers of the open sea and the risks of hugging the shoreline, they had been forced to keep moving along the coasts, where there was more chance of getting hunted by those unsophisticated humans who didn't realize the last of the cetaceans left on Earth were intelligent and cooperative creatures and not just meaty nuisances.

What you want from us Finnman? asked the scarred one, who answered to a set of clicks and whistles that translated as 'Defender'. He was pod leader, the oldest and most experienced of them all, as well as Free's potential new mate.

"I need those sharks drawn off, so they don't give the god warning. If you can do that long enough so I can get in and out of his lair, I will get the prize, and you can just swim off."

You swim faster than Dagon can? a female called 'Patch' because of a white spot on her forehead asked skeptically. She knew the serpent god well, having lived in those waters all her life. *He angry and cruel. Very strong. Dagon kills those who do not obey,* she warned.

"I have landwalker friends, and they will fight him for us. I just want to give them the thing that keeps calling to the fish people, so they won't try and come here anymore," Roan explained, which got the others chattering. No one liked Dagon, but they feared the warlike Atlanteans more.

Dagon bad. Fish people more bad, Free interjected. *Let's go play with teeth!* She said with the dolphin version of amusement, for that was how they described the raucous way the pod would chase the sharks away from a weaker member.

Teeth are big in harbor, another male reminded them. *Much danger in there. Not place to play.*

Free tipped sideways so that they could see the tattoo on her fin. *Much danger everywhere! I have marks from landwalkers for finding tick ticks that go boom! Many die; war is bad. Defender has teeth scars, boat scars, fish men scars, boom boom scars. Danger kill some. Danger makes strong those who live! Defender is strong, Free is strong. Pod is stronger! Fish people not belong, Dagon not belong, but pod belongs! We fight for peace! We fight to save sea!*

We fight then, Defender said with what sounded like resolve.

Fight the teeth, Finnman saves the sea for our kind! They called back and forth as dolphins surfaced to blow out and inhale a new lungful, before moving off. Defender led them forward, Free swimming not far behind him. Roan was imitating their rolling motions in the midst of the pod, hoping their flashing bodies would conceal his own as he swam rapidly along with them, heading back toward New Brooklyn Harbor, seeking to go into the flooded city and skirt the angry Lord of the Deep who was threatening to start yet another conflict between humans and the ocean around them.

~

Once all were aboard *Solstice,* including Jordyn Orion, David Shepherd gave the order to cast off. "'ow far out do ye want us to go?" Shepherd asked Jordyn as he guided the big ship out of the slip himself and angled her toward the harbor neck where Dagon's huge bulk blocked the way through the channel.

Jordyn was atop the pilot house, watching their progress with the Eye bouncing up and down in his right hand, thinking about all he must say and do. "Get us about two thirds of the way there, and keep your guns ready, but out of sight, unless he charges us. If all goes well, I'll have a talk with him first, for what good that will do. If I can't distract his attention long enough, you can always drop the charges as he comes in, and we'll time it from there." Blowing up a monster who considered himself to be a god was a rather radical idea, but trying times called for extremist techniques.

"What 'bout the lad?" Shepherd asked quietly.

"I'm still working out the details," Jordyn answered in an evasive tone. He couldn't set Willy free, for once he got that close, Dagon would sense him, and to bring the young man back to safety via the Eye would be to forfeit his corporeal existence. Jordyn still hoped that Roan would show up. Perhaps the agile Finnman could attempt an impromptu rescue.

"Sounds dicey, at best," Shepherd commented as he expertly maneuvered *Solstice* into the channel with a wide arcing turn.

"I'm a gambler by nature," Jordyn quipped, but in truth, he had mixed feelings about the entire affair, for he expected to hear about it later from the *Council of Infinites*, those ascended beings who were chosen to oversee that only the those who were truly gods had the power to influence the lives of mortals. Jordyn decided he would worry about that later, because he was far from the only offender involved. Dagon had brought this upon himself by setting himself up as a deity simply because he was huge, fierce, and quite powerful, and so was able to hold the Atlanteans at bay. Besides, the Council would perhaps be moved to forgive him if humanity actually prospered from his actions once the device was taken inland. Without the call of it alerting the Atlanteans to its presence and driving their urge to have it into frenzy, those offworld intruders would be more easily dealt with.

As they pulled into the channel and headed to sea, *Solstice*'s main engines fired and began to thrum. The big ship moved slowly toward the harbor outlet, and the dangerous being awaiting them. Jordyn disappeared into the Eye again, and the top of the pilot house stood empty, except for a certain inconspicuous little shipping crane that had been modified to toss things at a long distance.

Alfie Noble was below decks, feverishly working on a bit of a surprise of his own design. Vixy Macall had been drafted as his assistant and the inventive woman was a quick study. She had made small incendiary devices before, and so the design elements were not totally foreign to her—in fact, she was quite handy with tools. They worked together in tandem, packing powder into tubes, capping and waterproofing them before laying them in tarred casks full of shavings, nails, metal bits and pieces, before sealing them tight with wax.

Zephirine had refused to be left behind, and Jordyn had reluctantly relented to her presence aboard. She and Aleta stood together on the forward deck, silently watching the shoreline receding until the ship backed around and headed toward the sea again. The breeze around Zephirine played with both their hair, lifting hers and toying with Aleta's carefully groomed rows of braids. The smaller woman felt the uneasiness in the pit of her stomach begin from the rocking motion of the ship, and was glad she hadn't eaten in hours. She was bone tired—they both were—eyes dark circled and faces grim. The colossal form of Dagon the sea serpent god rose shining in the grainy light of the day, blocking all access to and from New Brooklyn Harbor.

"I'm getting tired of monsters and endless fighting," Aleta said quietly, and turned slightly glowing and troubled eyes up to her sister-in-arms. "When does it ever stop?"

"World is full of these things right now, from what I hear. We could certainly use more help," Zephirine said with a nod, her hazel eyes distant. Her hand was on the pentacle charm that hung from the silver chain about her neck, a long forefinger tracing the outline of the circled star overlaid on the base of upswept wings. For some reason, her mind wandered to the encounter with the furry humanoid that David Shepherd had called a freak. She idly wondered what had happened to him, picturing his speckled hide and soft brown eyes full of longing. Jordyn had told them that he had asked—what was his name? Roan, Roan Finnman. Jordyn had asked Roan to join them, but he'd not been seen since he returned her orrery, so was presumed to be uninterested. Funny how it all came down to the orrery.

What was that all about anyway? She planned on asking Jordyn about it later.

"I won't hold my breath on reinforcements," Aleta said with a cheerless laugh, interrupting her reverie. "Other than the crew, Alfie, and that shifty-eyed slut of Rushman's, I think it's just you, me, and Mr. Wonderful from here on out."

Zephirine nodded. "Well, we're getting our adventure cravings filled alright. Beats being a helpless victim like the rest of the world, I guess," she countered, as the colossal form of Dagon loomed ahead. "Time to head back aft, and see what we can do to help speed things along," she added, noting that Jordyn had disappeared from his perch atop the pilot house.

"I hope we get out of this one without more damage to Davey's ship," Aleta commented as they stalked together the length of *Solstice*, traversing decks now unencumbered by crates, the racks empty and previous battle damage still all too noticeable. She saw burn marks here and there, where she had charred mermen and pirates, and the memories of those encounters won after hefty battles made the small woman square her shoulders and lift her chin. "If we've got to do this, let's get to it. I could use a fortnight of sleep right about now."

"You and me both!" Zephirine agreed, stifling a yawn as she saw David Shepherd wave them below decks. "With any luck, Jordyn might head this off on his own."

They both hoped fervently for that as they climbed down through a hatch to see what Alfie Noble and his impromptu assistant had come up with.

~

Roan, within Free's pod, swam zigzagging through and around the underwater canyons formed by sunken, bombed out buildings that were once the magnificent skyscrapers of one of the world's most populous cities. This was the only way he could think of to circumvent The Harbormaster's blockade of the inlet channel, for while the water was deep enough there, no ship of size could cut through that area without grounding damage, and the serpent god knew that.

The dolphins thought nothing of these vestiges of mankind having been destroyed and drowned, but Roan could not help once again wondering what happened to all the fine people who had lived there. It must have been a busy, bustling place in its day, for far below were still broken bits of street, and toward the main channel were some signs of an even greater harbor. That humankind, who became so mighty they could build edifices that soared into the sky, could then fall to ruin anyway, was not lost on Roan. The mistakes that lead to the endless cycles of war must never be repeated. The Numen Orion had said just that, hadn't he?

Roan was lost in that thought when one of the pod squealed that sharks were closing fast, her sonar signals having bounced off several of them coming in from the left and behind. The pod turned as one, and spread out, facing off against the threat.

The warmer seas of the world had resulted in the bigger sharks migrating north, as much of the sea life below the equator had died off in the extreme heat. They had gradually adapted and became efficient coastal predators, always on the alert for movement in the waters they patrolled. While they were too simple minded to communicate with the dolphins or Roan, the serpent god could order them to attack, and their vicious nature made them good guardians of his realm. Even the merfolk were wary of them, and had not made many attempts to break through to New Brooklyn Harbor.

These were bull sharks, not huge ones, but as pugnacious and aggressive as their kind could get. They were more tolerant of the brackish, shallower water in the area of the flooded city, and were often found cruising there. These three had fixed their attention upon one of the smaller dolphins toward the rear, and were already trying to cut him off when the rest of the pod wheeled and took them on, darting in and out, trying to butt the gills and stomachs of the attacking bulls. Already, two dolphins had been bitten, and more sharks were on the way.

Roan was at a loss for how to join in the fight. He never wanted to expose his friends to this kind of danger! "What can I do?" he asked helplessly, lost amongst the swirl of bodies.

Swim away! Free's voice squealed in his mind. *We keep busy, you go on. We echo you later,* she added, and then went back to supporting her canny mate as he led one of the newcomers away from the path of the retreating Finnman.

Roan took a winding, circuitous route, swimming through many of the old buildings, most of which had no room for the really big man eaters. The small sharks he saw mostly swam away at his approach, but several he had to discourage with hearty kicks and pounding fists. Several times he exited a blown-out wall or shattered window opening to see a larger predator waiting for him, and had to swim back in and find another route. Twice jaws clicked uncomfortably close to his kicking heels. It was taking longer to get into the harbor than planned. He had no idea where Free and her pod was, and could not spare the time or take the chance to call them.

Having been down the better part of an hour, Roan's lungs were cramping, warning him he needed to surface breathe soon. In one building there was an elevator where the car had stuck on a top floor and he was able to follow the shaft upward, squeezing through crumpled doors a couple floors below. He spiraled upwards through the bombed out open structure, heading toward the light of the surface, when he saw the great tail wrapped around the building next to his. The Harbormaster was just above and to the right! If Roan surfaced there, he would be noticed.

In a panic for what to do, he looked around frantically. Nothing was accessible without a dive, and his almost empty lungs would not take that. There was only one recourse left if he wanted to breathe again, and that was to find the nearest projecting building, and climb to the lee side, out of sight where he could pop his face out of the water, and hope the behemoth god would not see or sense him.

Stealthily Roan swam over to a ruined building right behind the great body, and made his way up the far side of the structure, hand over hand underwater, trying to ignore the faint and far off calls of Free and her pod as they tried to locate him. If he answered them now, the Harbormaster would have him, and all would be lost. But if he didn't answer, they would presume him dead, and likely go out to sea again. It was a chance Roan had to take, as he was very near the surface. His aching lungs were about to collapse and if they did, he'd suck in water and begin to drown.

By sheer will alone, he pulled himself the last few feet over twisted girders and broken concrete crusted with barnacles and sea weed. Breaking the surface tension at last, Roan quietly popped his face to the air, and greedily sucked it into empty lungs. And then he heard a great roar of defiance, and a huge fist crashed down, smashing the top of the building next to him!

The Numen had arrived, and challenged the serpent god to catch him if he could.

As Roan ducked back into the water and swam away at top speed, the great body uncoiled and undulated after Jordyn Orion as he hopped and jumped from one building to the next. Away from the neck of the harbor they went, up the channel to where *Solstice* waited; her gunners on notice, and her impromptu catapult loaded and standing by.

Lord of the Seven Seas

Willy Teller heard a familiar voice whisper his name and opened his eyes. Turning his head as far as he could to the right, he could just make out what looked like that strange Orion fellow peering at him from within some sort of small glowing sphere.

"Can you hear me?" the voice asked, but it was more in his mind that his ears.

"I must've died already, or else I'm daft from drowning," Willy muttered through parched lips. "But yeah, I hears ya."

"Good, because you are neither dead nor daft. I have no time to explain this now, but what I need you to do, young William; is to watch me, and then follow my tracks around these building tops. You'll have to swim out initially and then climb up the off side of that first one to the north. Fortunately Dagon doesn't have much in the way of side vision! It's quite a leap for some, but you're a spry young fellow. Do be careful though. These waters are filled with hungry sharks and any misstep will likely be your last! Wait until Dagon is distracted by *Solstice*—that's the big ship we came in on—and then make your run for it. No matter what, don't stop until you get back to shore. Do you understand?"

"Yeah, sure, but I'm still tied up," the boy said, as the glowing globe skittered closer.

"I'll take care of that, but you just lie low and wait for the signal. You'll know it when you hear it because it will be rather loud," the voice added. The globe rolled forward, touched the rope, and it began to relax and untie and rearrange itself over Willy's body. Soon it lay over him in coils that were not actually circling him, so that he appeared to be tied down but was actually just lying under the rope. The voice in his head sighed in satisfaction.

"Now just lie here a bit longer, and when the real fireworks start, get going fast," the face in the little globe reminded him again, before it plopped into the water and bobbed away.

"If I get outta this, I ain't never pinching nothing foreign again, no matter what it's worth! This day's been something else," Willy said with a shudder.

$\sim$

Ever the clown, Jordyn made sure his official entrance was noteworthy. With a gigantic pop like a big soap bubble, he launched out of the water and exited the Eye in midair, landing lightly on a building top next to the irate Serpent God, who was startled but turned to glower at him.

"Surely you must have sensed me coming?" he teased, blowing Dagon a kiss as he tucked the Eye back into his shirt. "I made enough ethereal acoustics to wake Poseidon from his slumbers! Of course, you always were fairly dull-witted," he added in insult. "I should give *him* the Atlantean Star Tracker—at least he would understand how to use it. You're only a glorified demon after all, not a streak of celestial essence in that nasty, foul smelling, shipworm body of yours!" He silently thanked Aleta for the inspiration.

It worked too. With a bestial roar, a big fist came crashing down. Jordyn jumped away, and the chase was on!

He seemed to be headed toward the most tightly packed part of the sunken city, where Dagon's bulk would have trouble maneuvering. On every building he leapt to, Jordyn's fleet feet left behind a glowing bit of energy that would act as a track-way for the boy who waited for a signal

"Yeah, sure, but I'm still tied up."

that he was supposed to jump into the water and start swimming for the first building to the north. Jordyn hoped Willy could out swim any sharks lurking around that little spit of an island he had been held captive on, for he had seen some pretty big ones cruising around it. But he had a hunch that this boy wanted to live very badly, and so he would do whatever he must in order to get back to safety.

As Jordyn's race with Dagon began to angle toward the ship that was slowly approaching, he stopped dropping energy signatures. It would not do to lure young William into the line of fire. "He'll have to find his own way back," he said breathlessly as he continued to lure the rampaging demon god onward.

Dagon was quick enough to pick up that the Scion of House Orion was heading for *Solstice*, and raced ahead of the wildly leaping demigod to cut off his escape.

"No Orion calls Dagon demon! Dagon is Lord of Seven Seas," the monstrosity declared as he beat his chest with a fist, and lashed his tail until the wake threatened to capsize the big boat, which was riding high since it had only its ballast to keep it stable in the water.

～

"Ready on the launch, he's coming in hot!" Zephirine called up to David Shepherd, who was now manning the little shipping crane that had previously been modified into a bomb flinging weapon.

David grunted and cursed as he turned the apparatus first one way, and then another. Jordyn had warned him not to let the huge and powerful being get too close before he fired on it. "Why can't 'e just run a straight line, fer cryin' out loud? This thing don' adjust that easy!"

Alfred Noble rushed up to assist him, leaving Vixy with the last of the kegs to wick and seal while *Solstice* continued moving gradually forward with a lashed wheel. At least the majority of the fleet of New Brooklyn were either safely at sea or docked for the day.

Before maneuvering into the channel, they had warned the other ships to stay out of the water around *Solstice*, and so all the boats in the harbor were snubbed tight. A line of frustrated fishermen stood watching with their families, along with the crews of merchant marine, cargo haulers, and other ocean-going vessels, as well as plenty of onlookers and seal gunners; all crowded along the boardwalk on the shoreline, waiting to see how things turned out.

Many of them shocked and awed by the ferocity of the huge denizen of the deep chasing Master Orion through the flooded city, whispered prayers they hadn't thought about in years. The Harbormaster had never surfaced and spoken to them before in anyone's memory, and so the people of Yorkville had no idea just how huge and fearsome he truly was. Not even the team that had taken out the coastal pirates and downed the airship Goliath—which had in the past sent raiders well into dry land—seemed much of a match for this. Who could fight such a monstrous god and win?

Fortunately, Jordyn Orion knew a lot more about divinity than the average human. All things in the universe are energy at their core, and it is unto that they return when they have no more life in any incarnation. Gods might be immortal, but Dagon was no god, just a higher level entity that fed off the fear and adulation of his erstwhile idolaters. Like any would-be idol, the more he was revered, the more powerful he grew. Since he had not reached deity status, to interact with the surroundings the way Dagon did, that energy had to manifest in creating a corporeal body, which could be assailed. So while Dagon could not be outright killed, his body incarnate could be damaged enough that his energetic spirit would leave it. And that was the plan Jordyn had outlined, provided talking with Dagon didn't defuse the situation.

Which he knew it wouldn't...

No, in fact, Jordyn had not even bothered, for the negative energy around the self-proclaimed Lord of the Seven Seas was already very intense, and his mental acuity showed him to be fairly dull-witted. Yet Dagon was easily enraged and coerced into negative action; something that the Apocalypsians looked for in powerful lackeys. Guardian of New Brooklyn Harbor or not, Dagon had to go, before his brute strength and ability to navigate the ocean was turned against humanity.

When the Serpent God attempted to bludgeon him with a huge fist that cracked the wave lapped concrete top of the abandoned building Jordyn had just been standing on, crafty Orion sent a doppelganger of himself out to lead the sea demon on a wild goose chase. Instead of disappearing into the Eye, what appeared to be Jordyn hopped merrily from building to building, leading the furious ocean deity on a winding roundabout route toward *Solstice*. He knew Dagon would expect cannons or other normal shipboard armaments to be put into play, and certainly those might be used if necessary. But when the ship fired a single warning round and did not turn broadside to target him, Dagon ignored it as well as Jordyn, and swam back to take his position blockading the harbor. He never did see

Willy Teller clamber out of the water behind him onto an old building, and begin running and leaping for his life.

"Manchild dies now, for your folly," Dagon called to Orion's phantom image in a sepulchral voice as he lifted the rotten piling with the body tied to it. He opened his mouth for a big bite, and got the surprise of his life when Jordyn Orion himself, and not Willy, chucked a small electronic device down his gullet.

"Oops, sorry about that, but I thought you needed something a bit more substantial to chew on than a mere lad," Jordyn said with a wink before slithering out of the ropes to free fall toward the water. Confused at his double appearance, Dagon made a wild grab for him, but Jordyn disappeared into the Eye of Providence, just before his feet hit the surface.

A moment later, he stood beside a startled David Shepherd again. "I'd start launching those if I were you," he said, indicating with a pointing forefinger the direction of a very furious Dagon, who was bearing down on them. Jordyn hoped he had given Willy enough time to get safely away. The boy was important for the future battle with the Apocalypsians and Jordyn was loath to lose him this early.

"Aye, I will; but don' be spookin' me that way 'round such dangerous material an' all," was the retort he got as Shepherd expertly loaded the mechanism and lobbed the first barrel out. It flew in an arc that headed downward into the path of the rapidly approaching immortal and sank beside him right after Aleta set the short wick alight with help from a wind gust from Zephirine.

True to plan, the wick continued to burn inside, and the electro-magnetic homing device pulled it toward the furious would-be deity. It exploded into a burst of shrapnel that peppered his hide with sprays of iron bits and slag that were like a poison to a nether world being. They stuck there, draining bits of his life force away.

Dagon roared but never even paused, and continued to surge forward. Another charge followed, and then another. While the beleaguered Serpent God was gradually slowing, he was still very much threatening *Solstice*. If he got through their defenses, there was no telling what havoc he would cause to the shoreline community of Yorkville.

~

With the Harbormaster chasing the Numen, Roan had seen his opportunity. He took another great lungful of air and dove deep, heading directly for the channel and a sunken island he remembered below. Far underwater, his vision shifted naturally to selkie sight so the darkness of the water, somewhat stained by coastal runoff, was no problem to navigate. He had only viewed it once, but down there in the murky depths, encrusted with barnacles and other sea life, was the crumpled verdigris copper covered framework of the grand lady of the harbor. That was the Serpent God's lair when he wasn't roaming the sea floor.

The Finnman passed over the cracked and blasted pedestal first, jagged parts of her feet and skirts still clinging to it. The body of the lady rested on her side, her crowned head and the arm holding the torch having broken off, but lying nearby. Through the bottom opening he could glimpse something of an internal building structure, but it was unclear if it was passable beyond the part Dagon had hollowed out for himself. The remaining skirt formed a roof over a cave-like hole the would-be deity had excavated in the sea floor.

Several big and nasty looking Great White Sharks guarded the opening to Dagon's lair. Roan, peering around the base of the statue, was at a loss for how to get past them when something hit the water well behind him. Remembering Free's account of underwater mines, he was prepared when the explosion rocked them all sideways. Roan was able to cover his ears and duck his head between his knees behind the remainder of the statue base to avoid the damage it caused the unprepared sharks, which were stunned by the concussion. They now floated helplessly upward, unable to hear or otherwise sense his presence.

He wasted no time, darting quickly beneath them, and entered the chamber that Dagon used as his resting place. There were bones everywhere, some from hapless sea creatures, but enough human to make him sick at heart. Passing into the serpentine interior of the statue that had once been a spiral stairway, he had to half-swim/half crawl his way through, squeezing past parts of the structure that had been smashed during bombings or buckled when the colossal statue toppled. Now and then there would be an impassable area, causing him to double back and find a different route, and the structure shook ominously with each successive concussion.

Nowhere inside did he sense that part of the Atlantean device that Dagon had sequestered away long ago. The pull of it was weak, just barely discernible, and Roan began to suspect that what he sought wasn't in that part of the giant effigy at all. Perhaps Dagon had stored it in either the crowned head or the arm holding the torch?

As Roan was trying to make his way through it, a continuing series of explosions rocked the structure of the great statue, hampering his efforts to explore. Certain that he had not overlooked the device; he swam out via the armhole, only to be met by a rather large Great White that was just recovering its equilibrium. The big shark made a quick but rather lopsided dash at Roan, who swam as hard as he could for the head. It was closer than the severed arm holding the torch, which lay buried under heavy seaweed.

The old observation windows in the face of the crown were blown out, so he streamed in through the nearest opening, the jaws of death behind him clicking shut and just missing his toes. He dove behind a buckled railing, turning at bay, for there was nowhere else to go, as the back of the head had been caved in.

Fortunately the big shark could only get part of its snout within the largest of the apertures, and perhaps in time it would become tired of snapping at him and swim off. The more pressing issue though was his dwindling lung capacity. Roan had expended a lot of energy swimming hard, and his oversize heart and lungs had been well taxed to keep up with the need for speed. He was dangerously low on oxygen, and was beginning to feel lightheaded and disoriented. He would have to surface soon for a fresh supply.

In the open channel, the sharks would be able to follow him. Even if he got away from them, he might never get another chance to bring up the Atlantean prize, with the Harbormaster under attack, and the sharks wary of either coming too close or being temporarily stunned by the underwater explosions. Roan knew this was his best opportunity to become the kind of hero his mother had spoken of with great reverence.

The battle continued overhead. The bombardments were getting close enough to rock his temporary shelter. The shark backed off and darted sideways as a great tail lashed the water over them, catching the spikes of the crown and tipping it forward. Roan spilled out through the last window on the left, as with a groan of stressed metal, Lady Liberty's head rolled forward and fell on her nose, bubbles exuding from her ragged neck.

Roan swam with all his might for the arm holding the golden flamed torch. It had broken off at the elbow, and the only access to the interior was half buried in muck and rubble, which he had to dig through. The sharks had abandoned the area as the battle was almost directly over him, and Roan had to keep ducking and covering to prevent from losing his hearing or being hit by gouts of water full of silt and bits of stinging metal shards.

It was taking too long to dig an opening, and he was despairing of ever being able to access the inside when a particularly close explosion pelted him with debris, and almost deafened him. At the same time, it rocked the arm a bit, and the gap that he needed appeared. It was a tight squeeze, but he wriggled through, and made it inside.

As soon as he did, Roan knew he had found the device! A throbbing feeling in the base of his skull said it was somewhere just ahead. The original strutting of the arm was twisted and bent, and the limber Finnman had to twist and swirl to get through it, but eventually he made it to the fingers. His lungs ached and he felt dizzy as he crawled through the final few yards to where the prize lay.

Deep within the torch itself, shoved to almost the very tip of the flame, was a half-round disc the size of the big crabs in the summer-warm bays to the south. Even so long underwater, it had not dimmed or become inactive. As soon as he touched it, the pinpoint pricks of star positions lit up, shining brilliantly in the dark. As he ran his fingertips across it in wonder, it hummed louder and sent out a thin signal that any sea creature would be able to sense. But Roan could only touch it, not remove it, because it was wedged in position, just out of reach, caught between the barbed tines of a huge trident that impaled the skeletal remains of an Atlantean merman and then pierced the gold skin of the torch flame. Though he pulled and tugged, he could not remove the body or loosen the trident to get to the semi-circular star map. It was a painful defeat in the face of victory, for Roan's sight was dimming.

He needed to surface for air or he would die of drowning!

He reluctantly turned to go, but there was a set of ominous shadows at the far end of the open arm, now that much of the rubble blocking it had sloughed away. A pair of bull sharks had his only exit cut off, and he had very little air left in his oversize lungs. As they entered one at a time, trying to get at him through the fragile structure, Roan knew he would never make it out alive by going back that way.

With no weapon to defend himself with, he frantically searched for another way out, shoving against the material of the arm. In spite of the structure's corroded state, the torch end seemed more solid. He cautiously backed down the arm, desperately trying to break free.

A pad of seaweed gave outward, and something bumped his hand. Roan recoiled, thinking a shark had gotten through.

He looked up, frantic to escape. There was a panel missing overhead, and a familiar toothed beak was poking in the hole.

I find Finnman! The dolphin relayed in a set of long whistles and clicks to the others. It was the small male that had said he wanted to stay and fight, and he was not alone. The entire pod was circling the seaweed covered verdigris arm, chasing the sharks off.

Come, you need breathe, Free said, poking her head inside the hole. A grateful and exhausted Roan propelled himself up toward her and latched onto her dorsal fin, letting her tow him to the surface to save his energy for maintaining consciousness. His lungs were nearly bursting and the last breath bubbled from his nostrils as his face broke through the surface tension and he gulped and choked all at once.

Breathe good? She asked coyly after blowing out and in herself a few times.

'Breathing is very good," he told her first in human words and then in dolphin speech. "I thought I would die down there."

Free not forget Finnman, she scolded him. *Finnman not answer calls, so pod search. See teeth chasing something, think it you. All go now, god is angry, and he comes fast,* she warned him.

"No, I must go back to get the star map," Roan insisted, as he saw an obviously injured but still powerful Dagon bearing down on them.

Then go alone friend, she said, *pod not playing with god like pod plays with teeth!*

"Go, and thank you, I will deal with this myself," Roan insisted, as with a final deep breath he dove deep down to where the treasure of a lifetime was hidden.

∼

Solstice and her crew were making slow progress against Dagon. The demonic entity that would be Lord of the Seven Seas was staggered with each blast that went off, as the bits of iron that impacted his hide drained off the spirit world energy he had tapped into. His corporeal form had begun the fade and shimmer as he slowly lost his hold on the world of the living. He was a stubborn being though, and refused to back down.

Solstice was running out of bombs to lob at him, so the conventional gunnery was being brought to bear. Unfortunately, the range on those weapons was shorter, and that would allow Dagon to get within striking distance.

"Take us 'round slow-like," David Shepherd called down to Alfred Noble. "I'll be wantin' to chuck this last keg right down his gullet!"

It was the awakening signal from the Atlantean device that told the Harbormaster his cache was being raided. With a roar of defiance, he broke off from the battle and dove deep, racing after whatever marauder was stealing his star map.

"Damn, where did'e go?" Shepherd said in a frustrated voice as the ship came around and her gun ports opened. "Ready on both batteries, and look sharp lads and ladies. We don' want that big beastie a-comin' up on us unawares!" His real concern was that Dagon might surface beneath *Solstice* and try capsizing them.

That idea was not lost on Zephirine or Aleta either. They had a plan. "We'll need to hit him as soon as he comes up," Zephirine said, as Aleta bounced a fireball from hand to hand, her dark circled eyes glowing with the flames of extreme alertness.

~

Roan had just made it down to the metallic arm when the angry Serpent God came straight at him. With a huge bubbling snarl Dagon made as if to snatch at Roan, who backed off along the length of the arm, feeling with his feet for the open panel. He could tell Dagon was not at full power, but was still very dangerous. So were the sharks he called to his side like hunting dogs.

"*Thief! That is my star map! I should have killed you long ago, unclean thing!*" Dagon said in the universal language of intelligent sea life. Roan had learned that from his encounters with ocean going beings, and while he was far from fluent in it, he was able to answer.

"It's not yours Dagon, and it's dangerous to leave it here. I'm bringing it to the Numen Orion, and he will take it inland, where it won't call to the fish folk."

"*No! It's mine! I fought them all and won it from them. It stays here!*" he roared and lunged for Roan, who had just enough time to pop down into the arm and try again to yank free the body of the long dead merman before Dagon lifted the statue's disjointed arm and peered inside. "*You are dead now Finnman,*" he bellowed and began to tip the arm up, shaking it so hard that Roan had to hang onto the groaning structure or he'd land in that open maw full of dagger-sharp teeth.

Roan noticed Dagon's instability, as the would-be god shimmered a bit now and then, but didn't understand the reason for it other than it was some sort of energy shift. If he could just hold out long enough, perhaps the Numen Orion and his team might catch up with them. As the arm was tilted back and forth, turned upwards and down, the structure groaned and buckled more, beginning to break apart. Roan was shaken loose at last.

On his way out into the snapping maw of the enemy, Roan grabbed the only solid thing within reach, the long handle of the trident. He was surprised when it came free, but had no time to think about what to do next. Within moments he was tumbling out of the ruined arm, down towards Dagon with the heavy weapon in his hands. He did the instinctive thing and brought it around, barbed points first. With his weight on the far end, it plunged into the eyes and forehead of the would-be god.

Blinded by the weapon sticking out of his face, Dagon slapped Roan aside as he ripped it out and instinctively headed for the surface. He lunged out of the water with a mighty roar, thrashing and flailing about in agony, unable to see what direction his enemies were in.

That was when the Harbormaster of New Brooklyn, the demonic serpentine entity Dagon, met his fate.

"Fire now!" Jordyn cried out to David Shepherd, as he and Alfred Noble brought the little makeshift catapult around. Lashed by the waves created by Dagon's agonized movements, *Solstice* was rocking violently, so the shot went astray.

If not for Zephirine's ability to call the wind, it would have missed him altogether. But she managed to snag the barrel and when Aleta lobbed the fireball that would light it, Zephirine concentrated hard to split the air current into two halves, one to keep the missile on track, the other to make sure the little globule of fire hit the wick. It blazed hot and met the barrel as both went down into the throat of the enraged and screeching demon of the sea, exploding at just the precise moment that he dove back into the water to blindly search for his precious artifact.

Solstice heeled over a bit as the explosion beneath the surface created a surge and water spouted out into the air, soaking the deck. Aleta and Zephirine had to grab for the rail and each other to avoid going overboard. Fortunately the big ship recovered and while she did go off course, she righted and didn't take on too much water. The engines never missed a beat, and bilge pumps were turned on by the alert crew. As soon as David Shepherd could get safely down to the wheel, he brought his ship around and headed slowly back to port.

"Good job, team!" Jordyn Orion said jubilantly as he bounced down to the deck to find an exhausted Zephirine Merriwether slumped in the arms of an equally fatigued Aleta Kalama. He was pleased to see Vixy Macall and Alfred Noble dragging blankets out of a cabinet to wrap the two weary and drenched women, who had gotten the worst of the slop.

"Come below, we'll get a hot pot of tea going," Vixen Macall said with a wry grin, as if making tea for her former opponents was something she did every day. She had watched the entire battle carefully, and noted Willy's roundabout flight toward the shoreline, until a rowboat had met him and the errant lad had been safely brought ashore. She owed a lot to these people who had made sure Willy was safe from that monster of the deep.

"Will I ever have an outfit that doesn't smell like dead fish?" Zephirine grumbled to Alfred Noble, who helped her to her feet. On wobbly legs, she followed a shivering and equally shaky Aleta Kalama, assisted by a jaunty and ebullient Jordyn Orion, below decks.

"At least you can wash yours out. Everything I have smells like a smokehouse, including my hair," Aleta said quietly.

"Great. I guess we'll have to open a meat and fish market in our old age to justify the reek," Zephirine said with a melodramatic sigh.

For some reason, they both got the giggles over that, amid cavernous yawns. Battle nerves had begun to unwind at last, and the giddiness of utter exhaustion was setting in. As the red and orange streamers of sundown shown through thinning clouds, Solstice's brave crew were rowed from the sea dock to shore to meet a cheering crowd. Willy Teller and Vixen Macall were reunited as they were all transported into town, and given another heroes' welcome and feasted yet again.

Zephirine and Aleta begged off after a change of clothing, a quick meal and a drink, though Jordyn Orion seemed tireless as he told their story over and over again. Alfred Noble and David Shepherd made the most of the evening, but extreme fatigue and the battering they had taken overcame their adrenaline-spiked exultation. They also turned in early, though in separate places, for big and quiet spoken Alfie had won the respect, admiration and perhaps even the fickle heart of Vixen Macall, who just as quietly invited him back to her own digs on the former Rushman estate.

As night fell, New Brooklyn Harbor seemed serene, and for the most part, it was.

~

Deep beneath the gentle lapping waves, no one realized the fate of Roan Finnman. When Dagon clouted him aside, it knocked the wind from the half selkie, and he gulped in great gouts of seawater. His struggles to regain his equilibrium with lungs full of liquid went unnoticed as the demonic serpent god lost his battle to remain corporeal, for that final explosion sent Dagon whirling out of the world of the living.

In the dark, unforgiving, watery reaches below, Roan flailed around helplessly but eventually settled to the bottom, his brown eyes dimming and his mind slowly closing down as his body refused to find the strength to swim to the surface. His last thoughts were of his mother, and how badly he wanted her to know he had found his courage after all.

Ironically enough, the Atlantean star map was no more than a couple yards away, still attached to the trident and nestled in a bed of seaweed and ocean floor detritus. It was there that a curious dolphin nose prodded at it, as others prodded at Roan, sending despairing signals that traveled a long ways out to sea, and were taken up by other sea creatures who were native to Earth in that age. All night they guarded his body, chasing off predators large and small who might want a taste of the Finnman's mottled hide.

~

It could have been the corporeal demise of Dagon, or the reactivated star map stuck to the trident that brought another sea entity to New Brooklyn Harbor. Perhaps he came to find the source of the lamenting song of his ocean going escorts. In the late hours of the night before dawn, a misty fog covered the water. Through it came another fabled denizen of the deep. He made his way slowly from the open sea into the channel, guided by a pair of dolphins whose sea names translated into Free and Defender. In an open ship with no sails that made not a single splashing sound as it slipped through the water, he headed into the channel to where the dolphins said a heroic Finnman had died.

With his great shining sword laid at his side, long flowing locks, beard, and cape blowing in the land breeze, the god peered down into the depths and saw where the Finnman rested. A large hand reached down and lifted Roan's body to the inside of the boat, where the immortal being looked down with a kindly smile from a face that was ageless but infinitely wise.

"This is no way to reward valor!" a rich toned, accented voice said. He laid a single finger on the Finnman's head and concentrated deeply until the bleary brown eyes showed awareness and stared up at him without recognition or intellect. Roan was still dead, but his hearty spirit refused to leave his body, and so that part of the otherworldly essence that the learned call 'soul fire' still blazed brightly in his drowned form.

"I see you haven't given up on life quite yet. That is good!" the great bearded one said, and he smiled again, his voice a soothing sound, like the rhythm of the waves lapping at the shore.

Roan's brain was no longer working, and his simple spirit could not comprehend why he was still able to sense all this after death. He vividly recalled the experience of drowning. "Who... are... you?" the lips tried to say, though only the unformed thought was heard.

The gentle giant smiled. "Oh, I am no-one special. Some call me Manannán of the House of Lir, others the Old Man of the Sea, and I have many more names as well. But right now, I am your benefactor, if you wish to exist a while longer. Do you want to go back to the world of the living Roan? Or should I return you to your eternal slumber?"

"I... Oh, I... I want... I want to live!" Roan tried to say with vehemence, though all that came out was a thin trickle of water and a choking noise. The godly one seemed to understand nonetheless.

"Very well then. Now, to earn that new life, you must abide by my rules, and wear my sign always," Manannán insisted, as he ran his large hand over Roan's body. Warmth began to return, and thoughts like dreams came to his mind. Roan began to choke and gasp for air, and he coughed up streams of watery mucus as the big boat began to slowly move toward land. Mannanán Mac Lir continued speaking to him gently as the rocky shoreline of New Brooklyn Harbor drew closer.

"Hear me, Roan, who is a Finnman, whose father was the Grand Selkie Rónán and whose mother was a mortal woman. You are now under my protection and you will always have that, wherever you roam. Unlike the other Lords of the Deep, my influence knows no boundaries. You may walk the driest land into the farthest places of this wretched world, and you need only touch my sigil," he laid a gnarled finger on a silver pentacle pendant with leaping dolphins bracketing it that hung from a silver chain around Roan's neck, "And I will be there. Never forget that you are a son of the sea, but go where you dare, and I will be with you always."

The great boat came to a halt and the sea god Manannán lifted Roan's limp body and gently placed him at the feet of Jordyn Orion, who had been waiting for him.

"Well met, Son of Lir," Jordyn said quietly and reverently as he rolled Roan on his stomach and began to work the water out of his lungs.

"Well met Son of the House Orion," said the long haired sea god with great gravity. He crossed his arms over his bare chest, his long hair and cape fluttering in the land breeze before dawn. "I take it you are here to oppose the Apocalypsians?"

"Something like that," Jordyn said with a groan, as he turned Roan over and flicked back an eyelid. The Finnman lived, but it would be a while before he knew it. He looked back up at Manannán. "And what are you up to this night?"

"I came to retrieve Poseidon's trident." He held his hand out and the weapon of another sea god flew from the floor of the channel into it. "But then I saw you had lost your Finnman to the sea, and thought you would like him back. He could prove useful, wherever there is water."

"Indeed," Jordyn agreed, sitting cross legged before one of the most affable Lords of the Deep he had ever met. "By the way, that little trinket with the stars on it, could I have that?" he asked slyly, hoping Manannán had no designs on it.

In answer the great one slid the base of the orrery off the middle tine and tossed it to Jordyn, who caught it in midair with a tremendous leap. "Thank you," he said simply, tucking it inside his shirt.

"Just keep it away from water that runs to the ocean and the Atlanteans won't be able to track it," Manannán said gravely. "Now if you'll excuse me, I have other places to be and my people need me..." He reversed his position in the boat, which had no defined bow or stern, and it moved off silently again. A pod of leaping dolphins followed him out into the channel.

"Take good care of that Finnman," he called back, and Jordyn waved before sitting down next to a groaning and retching Roan to make sure he got all the water out of his lungs now that life was returning to his body.

The misty fog followed Manannán into the Eastern sky, where streaks of rose and peach sunbeams illuminated the water long after his boat was no longer visible. Jordyn watched him go, and then sat and crooned to Roan as he fought his way back to the world of the living.

"Such a strong spirit you have, to still be here after all you've gone through. Well, it's going to be a grand new day," Jordyn said to Roan, holding his shoulders up as the Finnman began to pitch and vomit sea water into the rocks and sand. "A very beautiful one indeed. A new day for us all," he added as he held a moaning and choking Roan's head. "Like being reborn, actually."

He planted a kiss like a benediction on the Finnman's brow between racking heaves and choking noises, noting with satisfaction the shimmering pentacle of the water element on a chain of braided silver around Roan's neck.

He planted a kiss like a benediction...

"And three of you found so soon! I expect we will be busier than ever once we leave this place and head off to find the last Elemental. So we have Fire, and Air, and now Water. So only the element of earth remains and the pentacle will be complete," Jordyn babbled on as Roan rid himself of the last vestiges of the drowning he had somehow managed to survive. "Yet I wonder where we should go to find that one," Jordyn said with pursed lips as he watched the sun rise through the cloud cover. Just a bit of its brilliance streamed through the perpetual haze that kept the skies a murky gray before it was swaddled in layers of cloud again.

He pulled the Eye of Providence from his shirt and sighted all around with it.

"Why we'll head north I believe," Jordyn said, helping a wavering but very much alive Roan Finnman to his feet. "North by northwest. That is where the wild country will be, and where it is most likely we'll meet our fourth member. Very dangerous up there, you know," he said, patting Roan on the shoulder as the Finnman staggered off next to his benefactor, who had tucked the Eye back inside his shirt. "But we have each other to depend on, now don't we?"

Roan could do no more than nod briefly, for he was concentrating on just putting one slightly webbed foot in front of the other as they tramped back toward the harbor town of Yorkville.

SILKEN DEATH

Broadway's Best

Jordyn managed to find them a berth on a fishing boat willing navigate through the drowned part of the city to where the land was dry again. It was a costly venture that lightened Zephirine's trunk considerably. She didn't grumble too much, for that was why she'd brought those odds and ends with her, though at the time she was figuring on bartering it for passage for herself alone, not four individuals. Roan offered to swim and save them his part of the fare, but Zephirine demurred.

"No, you should stay aboard with us," she insisted. "We know you can swim well and all that, but we need to learn to work as a team."

"I can work fine by myself!" he insisted. "I do what I'm told. But I get hungry and I like to swim. Swimming is what I do best," he insisted, his head hanging like a sullen child as he peered at her through dripping hair.

"Well, we don't always get to do what we want to, you know. Roan, you have to start behaving like a human being if you want to be treated as one," she told him, arms crossed on her chest and a serious frown on her face. He always looked at her like a lovesick adolescent when she scolded him—half hopeful but expecting to have his dreams crushed. In fact he looked at any female between puberty and middle age the same way because he had no idea how to act around women. From his selkie father he had inherited the most heart-melting, liquid brown eyes as well as an aching need to be cherished and desired. From his mother he'd gotten most of his insecurities and an eagerness to please. All that coupled with a vacuous though fetching smile made it hard to concentrate on how off-putting he was. And Roan was repulsive to a great degree in the atrocious behavior that had become his normal routine.

"What did I do wrong now?" he asked earnestly, and she sighed.

"If I had a few hours and the inclination, I could give you a list," she said with disgust in her voice. Always fastidious in what she did and how she looked, Zephirine had taken it upon herself to try and educate the Finnman. He left her exasperated most of the time. "You don't seem to understand how to act around civilized people! For one thing, you can't just stand there and gobble down raw and still squirming sea creatures, smacking your lips like that slimy mess was the most delicious thing you've ever eaten."

"Well they *are* delicious to me," he said petulantly.

"Fine, but the rest of us eat our food cooked and without all the grunting and chewing noises. And we come to the table fully dressed. Really Roan, you must put some clothing on," she added, trying not to seem as if she was ogling his lightly furred and somewhat dappled body, which would likely give him the wrong impression. "*We* don't walk around stark naked all the time, so neither should you."

"I wouldn't mind very much if you did," he said with something between a beseeching look and a leer as the inevitable happened once more. When Roan thought too long about women's bodies and what made them different from males, he always became aroused, and in his preferred state of total undress, the entire world around him was aware of his status.

Zephirine threw up her hands in disgust and whirled to walk away.

"Oh… just… go put some pants on already," she said over her shoulder as she stomped off, leaving Roan there, dripping on the deck and wondering what he did to upset her again.

"Must have been the squid she didn't like," he said, licking his lips over the uncommon delicacy. It had been a big one too, over eighteen inches. He loved squid and couldn't bear the thought of drying out all that juiciness by cooking it. "They have some strange ideas, these landwalkers," he added to no one in particular as he secured his collecting sack around his neck before he vaulted up onto the starboard stern rail, and in one fluid motion flipped into a twisting dive off of the boat named *Broadway's Best*, and went back to hunting for yet another meal.

Roan always seemed to be hungry these days, no matter how much he ate. He also loved to explore, for he'd never been this far into the old city. At least the bigger sharks didn't come into this shallower water. Many of the buildings here that had not been completely destroyed were mostly above water, just the ground floor and part of the one above it flooded out. In some areas people still lived in the upper parts, making their way down to the water via woven ladders of ropes, fiber, and debris. They generally used small rowboats to get around, and as in most watery places in the devastated world, hunted or fished for whatever they could, gathering salvage items to trade for things they needed. Roan was careful around these people, for they were mistrustful and quick to chase him away. Many were armed with things like handmade multi-pronged fishing spears and bows.

He loved swimming down to the old road level and looking at the rusting out and abandoned vehicles, road signs, mail boxes, and other debris, and wondering what the lives of the people who used these things had been like. Most of the items he saw were falling apart, crusted with barnacles and seaweed, sea anemones, shellfish, and crawling with starfish and crabs. Now and then he'd find a big lobster or an eel. There were plenty of fish, but not all of them were edible. Drifts of moon jellies bubbled around him as he swam on, leaving them to their business of scooping up whatever tiny life forms they consumed. Roan was looking for something else right now besides food.

He knew that Zephirine loved to collect things that she could later sell or barter to others for goods and services that they needed, and that Jordyn had traded away much of what she had to get them this boat ride. It seemed like an awful waste of resources, though certainly the others couldn't swim like he could, nor were they very good at catching their own food. If Roan could just find something that was useful or tradeworthy, perhaps then the tall woman with the pale skin and the soft brown hair that always seemed to be caught in a breeze would smile at him for a change. So he made yet another dive, looking for a building that might have lower floors underwater that had not been plundered.

It was surprising what exactly had survived. Most organic matter breaks down fairly quickly; iron based metals rust and rot, others corrode over time. Things like cloth, flesh, bone, and wood readily decompose. Even those long-abandoned relics of the bygone ages of liquid hydrocarbon abundance—plastics—had incinerated in areas that had been prone to wildfires or shattered like glass during the nuclear winters. Underwater, there were still some fairly intact pieces, but they were not something that sold very high, for they were plentiful enough even above the gradually receding seas. In the end all Roan found were some brass fittings and a battered AR mixed reality hard hat partially buried in what must have been a construction site. Well, it was something! He stuffed the fittings into his collection bag and with the hard hat under one arm, he sculled with the other to the surface. Roan took a deep breath of air, and spotting the boat somewhat ahead, paddled and kicked after it until he could catch the end of the Jacob's ladder Jordyn had insisted remain over the side and pulled himself back up and over the rail again.

He noted immediately that he was no longer alone, and began to tense up.

"Hey lookie here, the hairy freak is back aboard," a nearby sailor said as he elbowed another. Since there was little else to do without having to put the nets and traps out, they'd been lounging around most of the day, out of sight behind the fore and aft sails that supplemented the sputtering fuel-cell driven engine. The sailor who had spoken sauntered over, and stood before Roan, eyeballing him with a cheesy smile. "Didja find somethin' down below for me—or is it all just to buy favors from yer long-haired poofter b'yfrien'?" he added with a smirk, referring to Jordyn. His more dour-faced companion joined him after taking a quick look down the deck to make sure the captain was occupied.

Roan was never quite sure when he was being insulted, but he knew he was supposed to be polite regardless. So he stopped a moment and then said, "No, this is for Miss Zephirine. She paid for our passage and I'm paying her back for mine." He tried to move past the men but they got in his way, and made as if to snatch what he had in his hands. He yanked the helmet away, and instead, they grabbed him by the arms and Roan began to struggle.

"Well now, yer givin' that to me instead," snarled the bolder of the two in a low and menacing tone as he tried to pry the helmet out of Roan's slightly webbed fingers. "Hand it over ye furry beast, or I'll wallop ya good upside the head and toss ye overboard," he warned with a fist shaken under Roan's nose while his mate held the Finnman's shoulders and kept a watch out for the captain. She was currently busy in the pilot house, but if she came further aft to see what the commotion was about, they'd be in for it. She would never condone roughing up someone who was part of a good-paying fare, but these men weren't going to benefit much by that, other than having a lighter workload. They already knew that Roan was easily intimidated and he'd become the butt of their jokes and pranks since he'd boarded with the others. Other than ogling the two women speculatively, they had not remarked about anyone else but Jordyn. 'Master Orion', as the captain referred to him, might appear outlandish but he paid well and seemed to be intelligent and in charge, so they kept their comments about him quietly between themselves. The little man with the strange ways was sort of spooky anyway, and if challenged he had a reputation of giving as good as he got. But Roan had so little knowledge of normal human discourse that he often had no idea he was being mocked or insulted. These two had been the other reason he'd been so often in the water, for they tormented him mercilessly.

"Let go of me! I told you, this is for Miss Zephirine, not you!" Roan said in a loud voice, as he got into a yanking and tugging scuffle with them that resulted in the helmet flying from both their hands and bouncing across the deck.

Taking One For The Team

Aleta and Jordyn were just coming up the ladder from the lower deck, where the cramped passenger accommodations were. Her perpetual seasickness was better today, as the chop between the bigger buildings was minimal and there was little wind down at the surface to ruffle the waters. Tired of their stuffy and fish-smelly cabin, she wanted some fresh air. When they heard Roan shout, both raced the rest of the way up the last few steps and came out one after another atop the weather deck.

Again it was the same two members of the small crew that were hassling Roan. They just never quit!

Aleta quickly sized up the situation, and her eyes began to glow as her body heated up. "I'm not standing for any more of this!" she declared, and made as if to lunge forward, but Jordyn put out a restraining arm to stop her.

"What?" she snapped, turning fiery eyes on him. "I thought we were supposed to be a team who looked out for each other!

"Oh, absolutely!" Jordyn affirmed and he smiled slightly with his head tipped to one side as he watched the exchange. "Yet you can't always be so quick to intervene," he added with a thoughtful expression. "Give our Finnman a chance to work this out for himself before you once again rush to his rescue. To be a worthwhile team member, he needs to learn to depend on his own abilities, and that will never happen while you ladies keep playing nursemaid to him."

"Fine. But if they hurt him," Aleta stated with barely suppressed fury in her voice, as her eyes narrowed at the potential violence intended, "I'm holding *you* responsible!"

"I'll concede you that... but they won't," Jordyn answered in an affable tone filled with certainty.

"We'll see," Aleta retorted, unconvinced as she concentrated on calming herself so as not to burst into flame. Aboard a ship this small and constructed mostly of tarred wood, any fire would be dangerous.

~

"Now ye'll get yers!" The sailor's fist came up for earnest this time, and as his companion held Roan by the shoulders, he drew back to add power to the punch with the idea of silencing the struggling half-human. But these men had neither figured for how quick Roan's reflexes were or how slippery his short and silky, still wet fur would be as the skin it was attached to slid over lean and sleek muscles developed during a lifetime of swimming in cold water. Just as the fist came at him, Roan shifted positions and slipped from the grip of the man holding him from behind. He immediately ducked down and away, and the fist that was meant to flatten his nose caught the other sailor in the jaw, sending him reeling backwards before he went down like a fallen tree. While his primary opponent was off balance, Roan kneed that man in the groin the way his mother had showed him, and the sailor went down on the deck on his hands and knees, gasping. He rolled over and curled into a fetal position, groaning and swearing as he clutched his throbbing anatomy.

Roan snatched up the salvaged helmet and checking to make sure the string to his collecting sack was still around his neck, he bounded away along the railed gunwale and past the cabin area. He was feeling rather proud of himself before he caught sight of Aleta and Jordyn. He gave them a sheepish smile and stopped, hanging his head and expecting to be upbraided for his part in the fight.

"They started it first," he said with chagrin, not meeting their eyes.

Before either one could answer, the bulk of Captain Harding hustled by. Giving the strange trio a sour look that spoke volumes of what she actually thought of her latest passengers, she clomped up to where the two shirkers had been laying about half the day and began ranting at them in the dialect of the drowned city.

"Ye knows, I oughtta toss ya two sorry goldbricks over da side and be done wid it. I gotta schedule here and den' we're back to fishin', and ya messin' me up day and night! Now git up offen ya asses and onya feet," she said with disgust, reaching down and yanking first one sailor and then the other upright, and adding a shake to the one who had taken the chin blow. "Git yaselves down below and pump out dat bilge, b'fore we founder. And no tot for either o' ya bums tonight; ye've lost that priv'lege 'til I got some actual work outta ya!"

The sailors went on their way, with black looks in the direction of Roan and his companions. Jordyn watched them go, half amused, half concerned. Then he turned to Roan.

"You handled yourself well back there," he said in a low voice as Captain

Harding stomped on by again, her heavy boots making the deck sound as if a herd of work-beasts were passing through.

"Yes, you did. But they'll likely come after you again," Aleta warned him. "Be vigilant."

"I will," Roan said and smiled giddily under the unaccustomed praise, but then his mood turned somber. "They wanted me to hand over my treasures, but I got these to give to Miss Zephirine, not them." He showed Jordyn and Aleta the helmet and the somewhat corroded but still usable brass fittings. "It isn't easy getting in and out of those places down there. There's a lot of wreckage and glass I can get cut on. Cuts make blood, and blood draws sharks."

"And other unsavory beasts, yes," Jordyn said in a half-distracted tone as he was examining the helmet. "This is something we might be able to use ourselves," he said, tapping the optics and sealed power source of what was once a builder's holographic source of layout reckoning for installation. "That is, providing that the sensory parts within aren't damaged beyond repair. We shall see," he added, tucking it under his own arm. "In the meantime, yes, do offer those nozzles and whatnot to Zephirine, I'm sure she will want to try and clean them up for sale.

"Let's take all this back down to the cabin and lock it away, shall we?" Jordyn said with a sly glance around. "We wouldn't want to encourage further thievery after all. I'm not sure how much of our vicious Finnman these simple sailors can take!"

It was said jokingly but it still made Roan puff with pride, and for the first time in some days, he felt like he was actually worthy of being part of Jordyn Orion's team of heroes.

The Wilds Of Old New York

Their journey ended the next morning, when *Broadway's Best* docked at a rickety pier many miles uptown from where they had started. Captain Harding briefly saw them off.

"Ye said ye wanted ta head north, and this be the northmost dock, though not one we normally deals with. Good luck to ye."

She said no more and simply stomped away, issuing orders to cast off as soon as the passengers were ashore. While it was true that she had a schedule to meet with plans for the rest of the voyage back, she had other concerns about lingering there too long. What business this odd group had in the area Captain Harding cared naught about, for she'd already been paid in trade goods. She'd made it plain on the way north that this was a one-way trip. Harding wasn't going to risk her ship and crew on the behalf of strangers, so if once ashore they found the place too wild to be safe, that was their problem.

The four of them disembarked quickly, for one man was already untying the painter that had temporarily snubbed them to the dock and two others were back-tacking the sail. They seemed to be in rather a hurry to be gone.

By agreement they had left the trunk behind as part of the payment, for it was too large to lug around any further. Zephirine, Jordyn, and Roan had split the remainder of its contents—which were considerably less—between two roughly woven haversacks and a small backpack they had purchased in Yorkville along with dried meat and canteens. Aleta they had left free to haul what little she owned, for should she suddenly light up, any new material was likely to combust before she could adjust her flame to avoid it. She became their first line of defense.

"This is rather adventurous, like being the first pioneers into the wilderness, don't you think?" Jordyn chortled joyfully, but the only one who seemed as eager to explore the area was Roan. Aleta frowned and Zephirine sighed unhappily. They both knew from experience that Jordyn's idea of 'adventure' often turned dangerous.

The buildings were smaller here. Many were once well established mercantile businesses of one to three floors and the remains of older, stately homes, some of which were still standing. Beyond the docking area, which was obviously cobbled together in the last decade or so but didn't appear as if it had been used in some time, they were on solid, mostly dry ground. The land went uphill from what was now the waterfront so they took to walking on a badly buckled road that looped through the area, gradually going through the former downtown to where it was mostly residential.

They never saw another person. It was incredibly quiet for broad daylight. Usually any place remotely habitable close to a waterfront had at least a few residents, and while most of them might be out hunting and fishing, planting crops, or scavenging—all of which made some noise—there was no sign of recent occupation. By nightfall everyone was usually indoors, but it was only late afternoon, and not a soul around. So where were they?

Jordyn began to think something was drastically wrong here. He remained quiet as he mulled it over, his thoughts flicking between the deserted character of what was essentially now dry and potentially arable land that had enough intact structures and usable building materials to be desirable, and how little progress they were going to make should they have to continue traveling afoot. He fished out the Eye of Providence from inside his shirt, and scanned the area briefly. No sentient life forms were found, though there were other things present; mostly invertebrates from what he could discern, and scads of them at that. He looked around, puzzled. There should be wildlife here in the deserted suburbs as well as feral domestic creatures such as the felines and canines that humans were so fond of keeping as companions. Certainly there were plenty of plants, and the background radiation wasn't all that high, so there should be people scuttling about their business as well. Yet there was little sign of any of that—so why?

"This is a ghost town," Aleta commented sourly. They'd come to a fork in the road that climbed higher on both sides, and there was nothing much to see in either direction other than empty houses here and there between demolished buildings. There had been some rebuilding, but nothing recent.

"It is indeed," Jordyn agreed. "I can't seem to find anything living, unless you desire copious amounts of arthropod companionship, for there's certainly plenty of them to be found. Which also seems rather odd, if you ask me," he added in a cautionary tone.

"Maybe the people here are scared of us and they all ran off to hide," Zephirine suggested, but she didn't sound as if she believed it.

"No," Aleta said looking around them suspiciously, her eyes holding a faint luminosity. "Something else is going on here. We haven't seen as much as a rat or a small bird, and that's just not right." Some of the trees up ahead had a pale cast to them, as if they were sickly or covered with a filmy substance.

"Tell me, my boy," Jordyn turned and queried Roan, who had a selkie's heightened perception of the natural world as well as a lonely being's urge to wander off to where he could find acceptance, "Have you ever been this far inland?"

Roan shook his head. "No I stayed closer to the open water. I don't like places where there are–" he'd almost said 'landwalkers' aloud but decided that would seem insulting, "where people live who might think I'm a monster. I've been shot at before," he said and showed them a couple scars, one on his shoulder, the other on a calf. They were simply white lines in the fine mottled fur where a blaster bolt had singed the hair and skin beneath. "It hurts!"

"I'm sure it did," Jordyn replied in a soothing tone. "I know that your senses are more acute than ours. Can you discern anything amiss here?"

Roan glanced around, scanning the area, and he listened carefully. Then he audibly sniffed. "I don't see or hear anything much at all, but when the wind blows this way, something smells bad, like rotten meat."

That could be from decomposing bodies, though no one else had complained of a stench. Perhaps there had been a fast moving plague of some kind then? Yet they'd also not seen any remains, and with any kind of mass contagion, there were always those who stumbled outside in their delirium, looking for help before they died. Unless they had been restrained indoors somehow... Jordyn had a sudden dread about the situation.

"Can you pinpoint the source of the odor?" he asked Roan.

Leaning forward, the Finnman took a deeper whiff, and let his selkie heritage's autonomic system handle the input. "It's coming from up the hill," he said and pointed toward both of the road forks. "It's strongest where the trees and bushes are covered with that white stuff," he added with more assurance.

Jordyn had made up his mind that something even more ominous than sickness was going on here.

"We should investigate this further—especially since the only living things I've noted are strictly arthropods. So let's set aside our belongings and then split up into teams, and check out more thoroughly this malodorous area Roan has indicated to us." He left his own pack in a sheltered spot and the others followed suit. "You ladies continue on up the roadway there, and we'll head in the opposite direction. Call out if you find something or someone," Jordyn insisted. "And remain vigilant!"

He watched them start off together, and then turned to Roan.

"Come with me, because you've already been quite a lot of help, and I will need your more acute faculties to tell me what I can't discern for myself."

Roan was torn, because while he trusted Jordyn, he felt he should be protecting the females. "But... what about Zephirine and Aleta?" he said with the concern in his voice mirrored in his soulful brown eyes. "It could be dangerous up there!"

Jordyn patted his shoulder, which he had to reach up to do. "No worries, they're perfectly capable of taking care of themselves. But right now I need you with me. I want to further investigate this puzzling irruption of arthropods."

Jordyn didn't wait around but scurried ahead with the Finnman plodding disconsolately behind him. Roan went on reluctantly, because they were also getting too far from the water. That always made him uneasy.

An Unbelievable Infestation!

As they continued walking Aleta questioned Zephirine, who was gazing around with a perplexed expression. "Sometimes Jordyn says things that I just don't understand, and I wish he'd just tell us what he's talking about in the common tongue. What are 'arthur's pods'? Are they some kind of plant?"

"No," the other woman said with a chuckle. "*Arthropods*," Zephirine corrected in that instructor-like tone she usually took with Roan, "Are mostly small invertebrates, which means they have no inner skeleton. The majority of them depend on an exoskeleton, which is generally a segmented, chitinous shell, to stiffen them and keep their soft interiors protected. Some have wings but most crawl and depend on jointed limbs numbering differently depending on what exact class they fall into."

"Okay… so what *kind* of arthropods is he going on about?" Aleta asked again with an edge to her voice, because she couldn't quite conjure up a picture in her mind of what Zephirine was referring to, other than they were 'crawly things'. She didn't particularly like anything small with lots of legs because a lot of them could bite or sting and some flew right at you. Yet she'd not seen as much as an ant or a mosquito since they landed.

"I'm not entirely sure yet," Zephirine said in a distracted voice, because she now had spotted something very odd. There was a peculiarly shaped white object dangling from the sagging roof of a porch up the street, and whatever it was, it was fairly big. "But I think we're about to find out," she added as they increased their speed to a jog because Jordyn had cut through the area between the streets and he was motioning for them to come see.

"It appears that we've discovered what happened to the people here," he said with great distaste when they caught up with him. Next to him, Roan stared up at the thing hanging from the porch roof and he swallowed hard. Once the two women were close enough, it was easy to see what had upset them both.

It was the remains of a preadolescent child, all wrapped up in some sort of white and sticky fiber, except for the feet, which still wore a pair of handmade leather shoes. There was no struggling from the small corpse, it just hung there silent and limp; presumably dead. A fetid stench came wafting down with the slight breeze.

"Great Gods Alive, who would do such a horrible thing to a youngster?" Zephirine burst out in disgust. "Especially at a time when births are low and we're struggling just to repopulate this planet with actual human beings!"

"No offense Roan," she added, seeing the Finnman hanging his head.

"The question is valid; and the answer," Jordyn added with an outstretched hand indicating the wrapped child's corpse, "is not who did that, but *what*. Don't you recognize that substance, my scientifically-minded one?" He pointed again at the white wrappings, tracing the cords from a distance with his forefinger, starting at the body and then up to where they attached to the warped and cracked shingles above. They had a wispy quality that made them somewhat translucent and light enough for loose bits to flutter in the breeze, though most were about the size of fine rope. Yet they held the weight of the dead child easily and only attached here and there to the roof. "There's only one type of Earth creature I know of which can do spinning work like that on another creature's body, and only one substance that is strong enough to support it."

Zephirine knew exactly what Jordyn was getting at, but her mind couldn't accept what he was trying to tell her. "It can't be! There have never been any even *close* to that size before," she said with emphasis, though there was an edge of hysteria to her voice.

"Well there is now," Jordyn quipped with a frown, noting the blank looks from both Aleta and Roan. "What you see here is a typical arachnid kill, all wrapped up in spider silk, and the creature that did this must be enormous indeed. At least the size of one of us, and likely many times swifter and stronger," he added, looking around with interest. "Roan and I have already found several similarly wrapped remains in two other settings. I very much doubt that one spider cleared this area by herself, so there has to be others. We'd better find and eradicate them all, because if they have successfully bred, as I fear they have, there is the potential for anywhere from two to one thousand young from each female, depending on what species they originated from."

"You mean..." Aleta began slowly, looking around with eyes already glowing, "We have to hang around here to kill a bunch of monster spiders?"

"I'm afraid so, My Dear," Jordyn answered with a sigh. "If we simply leave them and move on, they will become a pestilence that will take over the entire temperate part of this land."

And that got Jordyn thinking too, because pestilence was one more sign of the Apocalypse. Was it simply an effect of radiation or chemical poisoning that was behind this sudden irruption of giant sized arachnids? Or was it some sort of meddling by a higher entity? Certainly if one of the lower angelic order was involved there had to be some sort of human intelligence that actually crafted the creatures. The lore of the Abrahamic Godhead had always stated that *he* alone was the Great Creator, and while he had tended to be rather stern and judgmental, he was more of the epic disaster type when aggravated with humanity. He had always left the biological tinkering to his beloved but often foolish mortals, knowing that at some point they'd thin their numbers out simply by tweaking the wrong part of the genetic code and creating monsters, which would lead to fervent prayers for salvation and ultimately more converts.

Which is what any deity was after, in the long run.

But now Yahweh was gone, taking his favored souls with him, and so his cleanup crew had come forth to begin doing away with the rest of humanity. Just *how* they accomplished that, Jordyn doubted that their leader cared overly much. These left behind humans were the descendants of unbelievers or the followers of other deities. Yahweh had little interest in any of them.

Samael had certainly wasted no time in seeing that the Children of Baal, the demonic slayers of humankind, were gathered together in one place as his army. So who had taken up residence in this part of the world, creating an experimental source of pestilence amongst the mortals?

That was something he would need to find out, but first they had to locate all of the creatures and eradicate them and any potential progeny before they spread further into Columbiana.

"We'd better get started," Aleta said in a hesitant voice though she was already aglow and had been playing with a bit of flame, moving it from hand to hand.

"Let's not be too hasty," Jordyn said, "For if we burn things indiscriminately, we might overlook some unfortunate individual who could still be alive. And I'm sure there are items here we could make use of."

Zephirine gave Jordyn a puzzled glance. "If we have to go from building to building to find these giant spiders, that could take days!"

"This is true," he admitted, noting that the day was getting on. "But I've noted that most of them are concentrated in this area of the settlement," he said and pointed out a rough circle about a couple miles around. "That should help somewhat."

Zephirine thought that over. "Most spiders are cannibalistic to some point, so if they haven't eaten each other they have to be a type who can live in social colonies. It would also narrow them down to mostly sheet web types."

Jordyn nodded in agreement, though he was only half-listening. "We should start here, because it seems to be the epicenter of the incursion, and then we can gradually make our way through the entire area," he decided. "This unfortunate victim," he added, indicating the child's corpse. "Seems to be one of the freshest kill we've located so far. That should indicate its predator is still in this vicinity. Most arachnids are nocturnal and have terrible vision, though there are exceptions, so I'm afraid we will have to go to them. Since this is likely a web spinning species," he added, indicating the area around them which was festooned with cobwebs old and new, "we must be cautious not to blunder into any of those. All are strong, and some are sticky, and getting free won't be fast enough to evade the builder."

"Understood," Zephirine said but Aleta only nodded, as she was still riveted on the little corpse dangling from the porch. "How do you want to do this?"

Jordyn thought for a moment, his head tipped on one side, and then he glanced up at the ever cloudy sky, trying to get a fix on the sun's position. "We've most of the afternoon left. I think we should split up again in pairs. I will take Roan once more, for he can sense things before I do. You go with Aleta. We'll work each of these streets until dusk, and then head back down toward the waterfront. I think we'll be safest there. Otherwise, as before, we're no more than a shout away," he added.

With that he and Roan tromped back to where they had left off.

Going It Alone—Together

Zephirine turned to Aleta. "Are you ready for this?" she said with a shiver.

"No!" Aleta said flatly, but her eyes were glowing and the heat coming off her was already noticeable. "But we have to do it anyway. Let's go see what is hiding in there. I'll go in first, I have the fire and the light," she

He indicated the cobwebs. "We must be cautious not to blunder into any of those."

insisted. With a small flame dancing in one hand, she took a deep breath and walked up to the building's porch. Glancing up once to make sure nothing was going to crawl down after her, she climbed the few rickety stairs and dodging past the area where the small corpse hung, thrust her hand holding the flame forward to burn off the webbing strands that covered the open doorway to the house interior. The spider silk refused to burn but it sort of melted, and it smelled strange, like scorched hair. That brought back some ugly memories for Aleta.

"I'm going inside, Zephirine, I don't hear anything moving around," Aleta called back. "Stay outside for now and keep watch, okay?"

"Gladly," the other woman said with dread. Regular size spiders she found interesting and knew they were important as predators. People-size arachnids were something else altogether! She kept her mind off the gruesomeness of the situation ahead by trying to come up with exactly what species of spider they might be dealing with while Aleta was taking the real chances. Some blackened shreds of webbing floated past and she gently blew them away from her with a raised hand. They smelled of charred fur or burnt cloth, she couldn't decide which. That made sense, for spider silk was protein based.

"Oh, gods no," Aleta exclaimed aloud and Zephirine was instantly alert.

"Do you need me?" she shouted and ran forward.

"You might as well come in, but be careful! The whole interior is a mass of webbing, and I've only melted enough away to see what's in here. I warn you, it isn't pretty."

Zephirine grimaced up at the little corpse dangling overhead, but she kept coming, for she could see Aleta's light. The fire elemental woman had placed a single flickering tongue of fire atop her head so that she could see well enough to direct small arcs of flame with her fingers.

The interior had been partially gutted to renovate it, and there was still some indication that humans had recently been using it as a shelter. There were bedding pallets on the floor and the scattered belongings of the inhabitants, including some tools. Just above human height except for the small area Aleta had burned out, was a rambling mess of webbing, with some sticky strands that extended down to floor level. The globules of spider 'glue' that beaded the strands were about the size of small melons.

"This is... incredible," Zephirine said with a mixture of awe and revulsion in her voice.

"This is a monster's killing field," Aleta said with a shudder, and pointed upward with one hand alight. Zephirine followed her gesture, and then cringed. With the extra illumination, she could see through the mostly translucent webbing to the grim scene above.

The entrance hallway had a high ceiling with a second floor landing, though most of the stairs were gone. Hanging from the railings and the old light fixtures were more wrapped corpses, and a few of the most desiccated ones had been cut free and allowed to drop to the floor below. At least seven people had died in that house at various points. No one was left alive, for in typical spider fashion, the corpses had been injected with a potent and ultimately fatal neurotoxin to immobilize them. Those that had been immediately eaten were injected again by digestive juices, so powerful that that their interior organs and musculature had liquefied and been sucked in like soup. Since humans have a cutaneous outer layer and an interior skeleton rather than a hard, chitinous carapace like insects, even the skin had eventually sloughed off and so nothing was left but the skeletal frame and the hair. Some of the partially dissolved remains had been wasted and the floor beneath the balcony was spattered with fats that had solidified, as well as copious amounts of spider fecal material in rather alarmingly large splats. It smelled horridly of rancid, putrid decay.

"I'm... going... to be... very... very sick," Zephirine said in a low and choked voice, for she was already retching and just barely holding back her gorge.

"Listen to me!" Aleta told her in a firm voice. "Focus on what has to be done, and helping me, rather than on all the nastiness in here. I need to know where this thing is hiding, because I want it dead, and soon. I'm sure you do too."

"Yeah... okay." Taking a few deep breaths and gathering her wits, Zephirine took her eyes off the corpses and the foul mess below them and studied the structure of the web. Initially her voice still shook, but as she pulled herself together, the knowledgeable side of her mind took over.

"This was made by a comb-footed spider, and a lot of them put leader lines out to the main web so that they know when something is caught. Those sticky strands are supposed to catch the prey." She had to compose herself again, because in this instance, *they* were the prey. "If you follow the web to the top, you can see it goes up to the balcony. That's where the spider will be, if it's still in here."

"Great," said Aleta in a sarcastic tone. "How do I get it to come out and attack me?"

"You *can't* be serious!" Zephirine said in a horrified tone. "These things have a strong neurotoxic bite even when their bodies are the size of a berry.

If something that size bites you, you will die in agony Aleta!"

"You let me worry about that," the smaller woman said with determination in her voice that she wished she actually felt. "I'll torch it long before it gets that close."

"They move fast," Zephirine warned her, but she could tell that her companion was determined to get this over with. "All right then, I'd suggest we need to rattle the web enough to draw her down here. They have terrible eyesight so they depend on web vibrations to tell them they've caught something."

"I already did that when I melted the stuff that filled this area," Aleta said with consternation. "How much more shaking is it going to take?" She was worried she'd have to climb up that web-festooned balcony to confront it straightforward.

"Spiders," Zephirine said thoughtfully, "will only go after things caught in their web that they feel they can easily subdue. They can sort of read the vibrations to know what's been caught. Otherwise they'd take the chance of being attacked and killed. So maybe the melting didn't feel right to it. We'll have to try something else. I suppose I could prod around with some air currents and see if I can tease it to come out of hiding," she added thoughtfully, though not without some trepidation in her voice. She fondled the silver pentacle charm hung around her neck for comfort. Its cool slickness and the wings on the pentacle reminded her that this was what she was born to do.

"That might work," Aleta agreed and then turned to Zephirine with an encouraging smile. "You know, I'm glad you're here with me, because I would never have figured this out on my own," she said with feeling.

The taller woman sighed. "I'm glad I can help. And no offense Aleta, but I'd rather be *anywhere* than in here at the moment! You're a lot braver than I am."

"Not really," the other woman said with a laugh that was mirthless and just this side of hysterical. "But what else am I going to do with this chance at rebirth and my 'wondrous' new ability?"

"Let's get this over with then," Zephirine said and with a deep breath she put her hands up and directed her will into puffs of air currents. She teased the overhead webbing right where the support strands connected from it to the balcony above, doing it in small amounts as would a struggling creature. There was a momentary scuffling sound above them and then...

Nothing happened.

"What in bloody hell does it take to get this thing moving?" Zephirine snapped as she moved a bit closer, ducking her slightly taller height beneath the existing webbing to target yet another area. The expanse of web was anchored in several spots above them, but they all lead up to that second floor balcony. The spider had to be up there. She wound up having to crouch underneath more of the web, and putting her hands directly overhead, she concentrated hard, blowing quick, staccato blasts of air that bounced the webbing up and down like a hammock. It was hard to not think about the floor right beneath her being covered in spider frass and the drippings of human corpses. At least the breeze she was making blew the worst of the stench away, though the skeletal remains in their spider windings lay all about her in odd positions, their now empty eye sockets staring through their silken coffins, their jaws open in final gasps of what was either terror or the struggle to pull air into lungs that were rapidly ceasing to function. Zephirine tried not to focus on any of that, but marshaled her attention on teasing whatever lurked above them out into the open, reminding herself that other lives would depend on her ability to remain focused.

"Something's coming down!" Aleta called out. Zephirine was instantly on the move, trying to scrabble out from beneath the web without getting any of the mess covering the floor on her. It was darker down there and hard to see, and she accidentally bumped into one of the sticky cords and was unable to yank free. Thankfully it only had a hold of her coat and a bit of her hair.

"Damn it, I'm caught!" Zephirine struggled to free herself. "This goop... is the stickiest... fecking... adhesive... I've ever... come across!" She became frantic when there was a thud on the webbing above her as a heavy body landed and began scuttling rapidly in her direction. She hadn't thought to jiggle one of the glue lines to entice the spider and berated herself for forgetting that. The web dipped a bit underneath its weight as the eight hairy legs and distended abdomen of an ebony spider as long as she was tall began descending through the layers. Even through the webbing she could see the red markings on the underside of the huge beast and she recoiled. In a black widow spider that size, the toxin would be instantly fatal.

She directed gusts of air back at it, bouncing the web like a cheap boarding house mattress to keep it away while she struggled out of her coat and left it suspended there, and then painfully ripped her hair free. She dodged quickly beneath the more open area as the huge spider swung itself underneath and crawling upside down, came directly after her.

"Aleta—*burn it!* BURN IT!" Zephirine screeched in fear because it was catching up far too rapidly.

"I need you out of the way!" Aleta yelled back, because while she could melt the webbing, the beast was too far beneath to be affected without incinerating her friend.

Before Zephirine could make it out into the open, Aleta let out a yelp of her own and whirled to face yet another menace with an arc of flame. Unbeknownst to them both there was more than one predator in that building. The second spider had been stealthily making its way down from the upstairs window, had crawled underneath the porch roof, and across the ceiling to where it could drop down behind them. It landed far too close to Aleta and she was forced to abandon trying to target the one stalking Zephirine and take on this new menace. She hit it full on with a blast of flame that almost set the doorway alight, though the large spider blocking their exit took the main brunt of it.

Aleta was panicked but her flame was incredibly hot and as pinpoint accurate as she could make it. The immense spider's exoskeleton was strong enough to withstand the heat though it began to cook the creature inside its own chitinous shell, and it began crumpling before her. An ominous gurgling noise, like the contents of a lidded kettle on too high a flame came from within it as its withering body writhed in the ongoing conflagration. And then just as Zephirine came barreling out from under the webbing, the carapace cracked and exploded, spewing extremely warm, smelly, and gooey bluish spider interior all over everything, including both women.

They had no time to deal with that because the other spider was right behind Zephirine. Retching and sick to her stomach, she still managed to turn in time to blow it over backwards. It was immobilized just long enough for Aleta to target it, and they both noted in satisfaction that as well as melting the webbing, the flames instantly killed the creature, boiling it inside its own shell. This time Aleta was more in control and as soon as the beast went down, she stopped, and they both dispassionately watched its last feeble tremors before it curled up dead.

All was quiet.

"I really need to get out of here," Aleta said with disgust, for while her body heat had burned off all the slop that had hit her, she was tired and shaking, almost on the verge of collapse.

"Sounds great to me," Zephirine said with loathing as she followed her companion out of the house and back out onto the road. "I want a bath—hell I want a power wash with antiseptic cleanser! But I suppose a dip in the water will have to do for now."

They headed wearily down toward the dock area, hoping that Jordyn and Roan would eventually find them.

The Team Reassembled

The road they had followed up and around this part of the settlement had turned out to be the same one as where they had left the women. It was all just one very long and looping cul-de-sac.

Jordyn and Roan together had done a cursory investigation first, and found no evidence of any live humans, though there had been recent occupation. They had found quite a few more remains, some of them suspended in trees, others inside or festooning the exterior of buildings. Because of Roan's more highly attuned senses of hearing, smell, and to some extent eyesight, and Jordyn's use of the analyzing features of the Eye of Providence, they were able to avoid the same kind of direct encounters with the adult spiders that Aleta and Zephirine had faced. Yet they also had managed to explore much farther into the village area, and discovered something Jordyn was extremely concerned about.

There were egg sacs in several places, so these genetically enhanced spiders had successfully bred. Most of the males had been consumed but a few lingered, smaller than the females and more wary. So breeding must still be going on. In some areas the hatchlings were already scuttling about the parental webs. There were hundreds of these newborn baby monsters, most the size of Jordyn's palms, and so quite capable of giving a very nasty bite. They might just die out as a new species if the town remained empty, but with the potential of roaming humans looking for a place to live, Jordyn decided that they had to be eradicated, and soon.

"Come, My Boy," he said, late in the afternoon, after they'd fully canvased the area. "We need to meet up with the ladies and see how they fare. I believe we will need an aggressive plan of elimination after all, and they'll be an integral part of that."

"What will I do?" Roan asked as they headed back around and down toward the area where they had last seen Aleta and Zephirine. "I'm not a fighter—at least not on land! And I can't burn things or blow them away. I don't have a star magic crystal ball either," he added, thinking about Jordyn's Eye of Providence. "I guess I'm not much use out of the water."

"Nonsense!" Jordyn insisted, and he rounded on Roan, catching his downhearted gaze and holding it with his own arresting aquamarine eyes. "While it's true that the better part of your talents lie in your ability beneath the salty brine, you still have skills we've yet to tap. In this instance, you are part of our early warning system. Your heightened sensory capabilities should allow us some additional warning as to what lurks here, and where. The ladies will be putting themselves in grave danger to do what they do best, and with your help and mine, we should be able to keep them safe until they eliminate this scourge from spreading further."

"That's important stuff too, right?" Roan asked in an earnest tone.

"Yes Roan, it's absolutely vital. It's why I chose you for part of my team. Not everyone has to be strong, powerful, or aggressive. Some just have to use the talents they have and be brave enough to face whatever comes."

Roan glanced at Jordyn with innocent disbelief but saw nothing in the expression of his mentor but reassurance. Gradually, through regular reinforcement, the Finnman's shattered self-confidence was beginning to rebuild itself, and he actually managed a slight smile.

"Let's go find them both then, and we'll keep them safe together," Roan said in a resolute voice.

"Now you're talking like a hero and a team member," Jordyn said proudly, and slapping Roan on the back, he went back to sauntering rapidly down the road, the longer-legged Finnman still having trouble keeping up with him.

They were discussing potential tactics when Roan stopped abruptly and sniffed the air.

"What is it?" Jordyn prompted him in a low tone.

"I smell that there's been a fire, and that something nasty burned!" He rubbed his nose and looked at Jordyn with a worried frown. "It's coming from down there," he pointed toward the area just above where the two ends of the road converged. It was where they had left Zephirine and Aleta.

"We need to find out what happened," Jordyn said with alarm and bounded away with Roan loping right behind him. Along the way Jordyn noted that many more of the unkempt lawns and shrubs were covered in webbing and that some of those webs had the crawler stages of the spiderlings lining them. They would all have to be eradicated.

When they reached the house with the hanging child's body, a very worried Roan suddenly ran ahead. He leaped up onto the porch and tried to peer inside, but the scorching, charnel house reek was intense and the burnt protein odor of the webbing proved extremely irritating to his extra-sensitive eyes and nose. What little that even Roan's keener sight could make out before his eyes began to tear up and his nose ran was right in the doorway. The desiccated corpse of a very large spider lay crumpled in death, its abdomen blasted apart. He backed off and let Jordyn push past him to peer inside as well—extending one hand with the Eye lit up like a torch.

"Well, this is interesting, in rather a stomach churning way," Jordyn said as he backed out again.

"That's just plain nasty!" Roan said, wiping slightly webbed hands over his eyes and nose as he blundered back off the sagging porch. "Do you think they're still in there? Are they... dead?"

Jordyn still had his Eye out, and he was scanning the house and the area around it. "If you mean our female team members, no," he said. "They're neither alive nor dead inside, I can at least confirm that because their soul signatures are still quite distinct. But this is Aleta's work for certain, so they have been here. In fact," he added, turning slowly so that the Eye scanned well ahead, "I'm getting two very much animate transcendent human life forms down at the dock area. Unless we have some similarly supremely-enhanced visitors, I would wager that our companions headed down there for a bit of a wash, seeing as they've blown up at least one spider that we know of." He bounded off the porch and began heading down the road, Roan trotting right behind him.

"I wish I could wash that stink right out of my nose!" Roan quipped. "I've smelled rotten fish that weren't that bad."

But Jordyn wasn't really listening to Roan's complaints; he was too busy scanning as they went along. There was no arthropod activity in the lower part of the area, just up in the residential section. So perhaps they were fortunate enough to be able to contain the irruption here. He really need-ed to speak to Zephirine about that, she'd know more details about Earth spiders than he would.

~

They met up later, and once the ladies felt clean and Roan had a swim, they all collected some driftwood and old boards to build a fire. While the women changed to dry clothing, Roan brought them fish and mussels to steam in seaweed, though he sat aside and ate his raw, trying not to grunt and slurp aloud. He'd also conceded to at least wear a pair of slacks and some handmade sandals that Zephirine had traded for and been nagging him about for weeks. It felt odd to don human clothing again, but Roan wanted to be thought of as a team member now.

The night air was cold, and they'd have to sleep outdoors to be safe. At least their bags were safely stowed away down by the docks, and with no one in the area, they'd remain there until needed, after the cleansing was over with.

"If these adult spiders are any indication," Zephirine told them as they sat around the fire before bedding down, "They're following typical black widow behavior. They aren't leaving their hiding spots and just catching what they can. I'm sure people wander in here from time to time."

"So they won't spread?" Jordyn asked curiously, and Zephirine took a moment to think it over.

"The adults likely won't, but the young certainly can. In fact that's what worries me most about this situation! You see, when spiders are over-crowded at hatching, first they cannibalize one another, then they migrate so that at least some of the young survive. Each egg case of a Black Widow contains hundreds of eggs. While many of those hatchlings won't survive, enough will. The cannibalism usually results in the best and strongest hunters remaining, but then they have to find new territory. That's usually accomplished through ballooning, since they can't very well walk to the next inhabited area."

Aleta looked confused. "How do they 'balloon'? It's not like blowing up, is it? That killed those two big ones."

"No," Zephirine said with an uncomfortable grimace, for she'd had to scrub to get the dead spider goop off her clothing, skin, and out of her hair, and she still didn't feel clean enough. The water here was brackish and not as salty, but without soap, she'd done the best she could with sand and reeds to abrade it off her. Her fair skin was still pink and sore. "Ballooning is when spiders find a high spot, point their behinds in the air, and let out enough silk to allow them to float off. They can go quite a distance before they land."

"We saw hatchlings in some areas," Jordyn said in a serious tone. "Hundreds of them! We can't let that happen."

"Then we have to act fast," Zephirine insisted. "We have to burn off the entire area."

"Not tonight," Aleta begged. "I'm just too worn out."

"Let's get some sleep then," Jordyn insisted. "At least those of you who need it. I don't, so I will remain awake and keep watch."

No one was about to argue with him on that. The remaining three settled down on the sand and tried to get comfortable. They eventually rolled together and slept like puppies, using each other's bodies for warmth.

Roan was very excited about that, but he forced himself to remain in control. He was part of a team now.

Requiem For A Town Of The Dead

The dawn came early, and even though the sun could not poke through the ever-present clouds, little fingers of its light gilded the horizon. They rose early, and with only sips of fresh water and a few bites of the dried meat they'd brought along, the quartet of monster slayers headed uptown.

"How do you want to handle this?" Aleta asked Jordyn as they stopped at the fork that marked the cul-de-sac that seemed to be the epicenter of the behemoth black widows.

He thought for a moment. "Most of this area is filled with wood and that will burn. We'll have to ring it with fire and then perhaps Zephirine can blow it inwards." It sounded reasonably accomplishable to him.

"Any stray breeze could spread this thing you know," Zephirine said with a frown.

Jordyn turned to her. "Can't you deaden the wind as well as cause it to blow harder?" he asked her with a raised eyebrow and a smirk.

She stared at him, temporarily speechless. "I never tried! All I ever did was adjust it for the boats and ships. I suppose I could attempt to block it somehow," she added thoughtfully. "Or at least cause it to blow inward."

"That would help," Aleta decided. "I'll handle the fire, you keep the wind turned in, and Roan will..."

"I'll watch for spiders escaping," he said with confidence, and brandished a long piece of boat strake. "I can whack anything that gets away."

"There you have it!" Jordyn chortled happily. "Our first team effort involving our Finnman on land."

～

And that's how it basically went, though it took most of the day and well into the evening to burn out the entire area. Aleta kept her fire going, and once the old houses, the wooden rubble, and the plants began to burn, spiders of all sizes and both sexes boiled out of their hiding places and tried to scramble away. Not a single one of the adults got through the blaze and the smoke and cinders swirled up in a tight spiral. Any young spiders that tried ballooning to escape found themselves whirled around and back downward into that noxious conflagration until they perished as well. There were explosions both large and small, as spider bodies popped all over the place.

"Why are the spider's insides blue?" Roan wanted to know, and Aleta glanced at him with disgust.

"Yuck! Who cares?" she snapped and moved off to keep another area burning.

"Their rudimentary circulatory system is based on copper, not iron like ours," Zephirine told him without looking away from her own business of keeping the fire as compact in the area as possible. "Iron makes red blood cells. Copper blood tends to be bluish."

"That's pretty interesting," he said and almost added that he wondered if they were good to eat, like crabs and lobsters, which also had blue blood, at least when raw. He recalled in time that Zephirine had repeatedly said that watching him eat live creatures was stomach-turning. Besides, these spiders were now all cooked and would be rubbery.

By nightfall, all of the spiders they could find were dead or dying, and any webs or egg cases had melted into woolly slag. That residential area was no more than charred timbers and whatever metals or concrete hadn't melted. Nothing lived there anymore, according to Jordyn.

Zephirine was able to direct dust devils of sand and waterspouts from the dock area to help extinguish the flames. She ringed the area with water, though no doubt the former settlement would remain hot for some time. Jordyn and Roan toured around the rest of the town just before sundown, and neither the Finnman's acute senses or the Eye of Providence found anything amiss.

$\sim$

"I believe they've all perished," Jordyn announced later to the tired little trio down at the docks that evening. "Once again, you three have made me proud, for you've proved yourselves the champions of humankind. Had they spread, such an apex predator would have become a scourge that might eventually have wiped out all the remaining people in this temperate part of the continent. You have also given those poor souls who died back there some release from their Earthly torment by adding meaning to their sacrifice. At some time in the future, this area should be deemed safe for habitation again."

"Yay us," said Aleta tiredly. "Now where do we go from here?"

Jordyn took no offense to her flippant attitude—he could tell Aleta was exhausted. He focused on answering her question about what would be their next destination, for he had thought that over considerably the night before, as he'd sat awake, keeping watch while the others slept.

"We will all move on tomorrow, for there's far more to learn as we explore. You three should get a good sleep tonight, for I doubt you'll be bothered here. Your Finnman will know if something is wrong, so learn to trust him." He smiled at Roan, who nodded agreeably. "You'll be heading north in the morning. Stick together."

Zephirine looked up from picking away at her meal of roasted fish. "What about you?" she asked sharply, as Jordyn took out his Eye of Providence and stood up.

"I am going to scout ahead and get a look at this land we're in. This little interlude tells me that there's far more going on here than it seems from our perspective. I'll meet with you again as soon as I know where we should head next. Don't worry—I can find you anywhere, for you are all one of a kind!" he added brandishing the Eye. "And be assured, you're all perfectly capable of handling yourselves in any situation that might arise."

And with that, he simply reabsorbed back into the Eye of Providence, and zipped away, like a glowing soap bubble in the sky.

THE END

ABOUT OUR CREATORS

WRITER –

NANCY HANSEN - An avid reader and prolific writer of fantasy and adventure fiction for over 30 years, Nancy A. Hansen is the author of many novels, anthologies, and short stories. You can find some of her work at Pro Se Press where she has a selection of original offerings of novel length under her imprint *HANSEN'S WAY*, as well as numerous short stories that have been contributed to various Pro Se multi-author publications. She also shares a children's adventure series called *Companion Dragons Tales* with co-authors Roger Stegman and Lee Houston Jr.

At Airship 27, Nancy has contributed short stories to *Sinbad-The New Voyages* and *Tales From The Hanging Monkey* anthologies, and she has an ongoing series of the very popular *Jezebel Johnston* pirate novels, including a 4 book omnibus. She also contributed to the Airship 27 anthology, *Legends of New Pulp Fiction*.

Nancy has also written for Mechanoid Press in their *Monster Earth* debut anthology, and at Flinch Books contributed to *Restless: An Anthology of Mummy Horror*. Nancy also has a story in the charity anthology *Lost Children*, which benefits groups that help abused and exploited youngsters.

Nancy has an Amazon Author Page at https://www.amazon.com/Nancy-Hansen/e/B009OGK632/ref=dp_byline_cont_ebooks_3

Her books are also available on Barnes & Noble online and some on Smashwords.

Nancy currently resides on an old farm in beautiful, rural eastern Connecticut with an eclectic cast of family members, and one very spoiled dog.

COVER ARTIST AND INTERIOR ILLUSTRATOR

G.S.Davis - is an artist hailing from the wilds of Arvada. At the tender age of 15, he discovered that his calling was storytelling. Naturally he discovered this talent while trying to get out of trouble with his mother. As time went on, he evolved his talent and soon began writing comics. Now, many years later, he's still trying to avoid getting in trouble, though he believes that his wife is probably on to him at this point. So he tends to hide in his office, writing comics and putting them out into the world. He draws in two different styles: A cartoon style distantly reminiscent of the newspaper strips of yore, and a more serious Manga style, distantly reminiscent of Japanese comic books from that far away land.

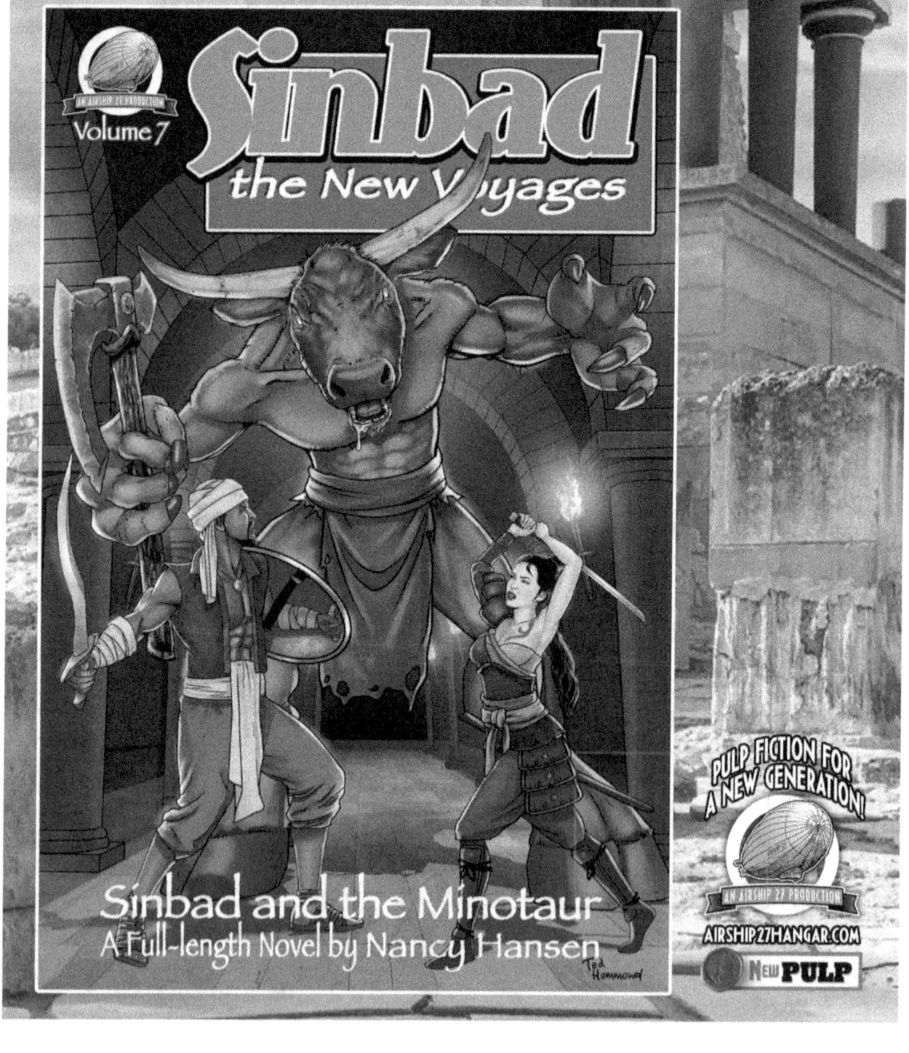